ADVICE FROM AN OLD-TIMER

Hodig scratched his grizzled head as he looked at the hard, dark, intense man called Rafe Dolan.

"You asked me how to take Bronc Farrel and his crew?" Hodig said. "Well, son, I'll tell you. I've been around here long enough to see the way Farrel operates. And the only way you're going to beat him is play it the way he does. Get yourself a bunch of the best guns in the territory, swoop down on him, and blast him and his men off the face of the earth."

"That's just about how I figured it," Dolan said. What he didn't say was, he couldn't afford any hired guns. And that left him with one choice.

Alone, he would have to do the work of an army of gunfighters.

BUCKSKIN MAN

WAYNE D. OVERHOLSER

A DELL BOOK

Published by
DELL PUBLISHING CO., INC.
750 Third Avenue
New York, New York 10017

Dell ® TM 681510, Dell Publishing Co., Inc.
Manufactured in The United States of America
First Printing—August 1969

BUCKSKIN
MAN

CHAPTER 1

HE RODE EAST across south-central Oregon, a hard-muscled, long-boned man with a face burned almost to Indian bronze by sun and wind. His Shoshoni friends called him a variety of names, the Bull or the Coyote or the Cougar; a few who were not his friends called him Son-of-a-Bitch-Who-Has-a-Sharp-Knife.

According to his baptismal record, his name was Rafael Socrates Dolan. The combination of names made no sense, the baptism was long forgotten, and to his white friends he was simply Rafe Dolan.

He wore a buckskin suit darkened by dirt and age, a broad-brimmed black hat with two bullet holes in the crown, and a pair of beaded moccasins. He carried a knife in a scabbard on his left side, a .45 Colt in a holster on his right side, and he had a Winchester in the boot.

Dolan had one guiding principle: a man had the right to live without restraints on his personal liberty. It was a principle he was willing to fight for, and on more than one occasion he had. To paraphrase Daniel Boone, Dolan believed that when a man smelled his neighbor's privy or pigpen, it was time to move on.

The Cascade Range was behind him: Steens Mountain was ahead. He swung south around Lake Abert; he had to swing still farther south to find a way to the rim. He crossed dry lake beds with their smell and feel of death; he saw thousands of bones bleached white under the brilliant sun, antelope and deer and maybe buffalo, although buffalo had been gone from this part of the country for most of the century.

The sagebrush was all around him, with here and there the dark green of a wind-twisted juniper. In general the land was flat or rolling, but the horizon was cut by a number of buttes, and occasionally he found himself coming up against a stretch of rimrock that delayed him until he found a tortuous route to the top.

He followed no road and no trail; he camped when he found water. He had no deadline in time; he never put in a hard day, so when he reached the end of his journey, his sorrel gelding and pack animal were in good shape.

On an afternoon in late June he caught his first glimpse of white-capped Steens Mountain, the peaks so much like clouds nestling along the horizon that at first he wasn't sure he was actually seeing the mountain. He had ridden along the eastern side of Steens Mountain last fall. He had been reminded of the Rockies, the pointed, jagged peaks dropping a sheer three thousand feet or more to the sage flat at their base.

On the western side the mountain was entirely different. The slope lifted in a long, gradual slant to the top, perfect hunting, he thought. A second thought brought a sour taste to his mouth. On this side the mountain would furnish the finest cattle graze in the world. If the cows weren't here yet, they would be, and with them would come the arbitrary law of the cattlemen. He'd had some experience with both the cattlemen and their law, and he hated them.

Before sundown the next day he crossed a road of sorts, twin ruts running north and south through the sage. A short time later he reached the base of the mountain and stopped beside a spring which gushed out of the cracks in the rocks at the base of a fifty-foot cliff and gave birth to a swift-flowing creek that rushed northward. He let his horses drink; he dropped flat on his belly upstream from them and drank. The water was sweet and cold, the best water he'd had since he'd left the Cascades.

He mounted and rode north along the creek for a mile or more until he reached a grove of cottonwoods. He dismounted with a sigh of relief, for it had been a long ride across an empty and desolate land. He staked out his sorrel and pack animal, and as he looked around, he told himself he would never find a better campsite than this.

Here was water and wood and grass for the horses. He had seen hundreds of antelopes since morning and there would be deer on the mountain and trout in the creek. Why, a man could camp here all summer and live off the land, and not have to ride more than a mile from this very spot.

As far as Dolan knew, there were no towns within one hundred miles. He wasn't sure what ranches were in the country, but so far he had seen no cows and no horses and no trace of humans. This was the place he had been looking for, so why not stay?

He needed nothing except ammunition, coffee, salt, and smoking tobacco. There must be a store or trading post somewhere within a day's ride. If he ran short of shells, he'd explore the country until he found such a store.

He gathered several armloads of dead limbs and dropped them beside the creek. He built a fire and, straightening, turned to see three riders emerge from a steep-walled canyon. They saw him and reined toward him.

Dolan sighed. He had never been a man to hunt trouble, but through most of his twenty-nine years it had seemed that trouble had hunted him. One horseman moved out ahead of the other two. He would be the boss man, perhaps the foreman of some nearby spread, a familiar type, the kind of cowman who made Dolan hate all ranchers and cowboys.

This was unfair and Dolan knew it. The trouble was he tended to forget the friendly ones he had run into. The others were the ones he remembered, the overbearing, domineering bastards who thought they owned the public domain and who made their own law in a land where there had been no law.

This fellow was big with a bristling yellow moustache and pale-blue eyes. His nose was short with flaring nostrils. He wore a calfskin vest and a gun on each hip, and when he reined up twenty feet from Dolan and dismounted, it seemed to Dolan that the black gelding the man had been riding straightened his back and took a breath of relief.

For a time the fellow stood motionless, his gaze moving slowly down Dolan's long body from his broad-brimmed hat to his beaded moccasins and back up again, a derisive grin on his thick lips. He made it plain that he wanted Dolan to feel his contempt. Dolan did, and his anger began to stir.

He shot a quick glance past the man in front of him to the other riders. They were dark-skinned with bushy moustaches. Mexicans, Dolan told himself, and remembered hearing that the cowmen who lived around Steens Mountain had come north from California with their herds and had brought their vaqueros with them.

Dolan turned his gaze back to the big man. He ran a little too much to fat and an overlarge belly. Dolan had a notion that the cowman was usually able to overpower others by his size and domineering manner. That done, he had won half his battle, but Rafe Dolan had never in his life been overpowered by either a man's size or his domineering manner, so he stood motionless, meeting the fellow's stare.

The silence ran on and on until it was almost unbearable, and then, apparently thinking he had achieved his purpose, the man said, "I'm Pete Larkin. I ramrod F Ranch." He jerked a thumb to the north. "It's five miles from here. Belongs to Bronc Farrel. Ever hear of him?"

"No," Dolan said. "I never heard of F Ranch or you, either."

"You're hearing of them now," Larkin said arrogantly. "Who are you?"

"My name's Dolan."

"What are you doing here?"

"Camping."

"Why?"

"I like the place," Dolan answered.

"You're trespassing on F Ranch range," Larkin said as if he were giving an order to someone he considered inferior. "Be gone by sunup."

Larkin turned to his horse as if he had no doubt that he would be obeyed. He started to lift a booted foot to a stirrup when Dolan said clearly, "You can go to hell. I'm staying."

Larkin's foot came down to the ground and he wheeled away from his horse, his dark face turning darker until it was almost purple. He stared at Dolan as if he had committed sacrilege and he couldn't believe he had heard right.

"I told you to slope out of here," Larkin said. "If we find you here in the morning, you'll swing from one of them limbs." He motioned toward the nearest cottonwood. "We don't allow saddle bums to camp on F Ranch range."

"I figure this is public domain," Dolan said, "and I don't let any god-damned tub of lard order me off of it."

For a moment Larkin stood frozen, his lips parted in shocked surprise, then he drove at Dolan, a big fist swinging up from his knees that would have knocked any man cold if it had landed. Dolan simply tipped his head to one side, the fist slipped by without touching him, and Larkin was turned partly around by the force of the blow.

The man was off balance and completely defenseless for an instant. Dolan took one short step forward and hit Larkin on his jaw with a driving fist. The sound was that of a butcher's meat cleaver striking a side of beef. Larkin staggered back, his arms flying up, and he sprawled full length on the ground.

Dolan fell on him, his knees striking Larkin in his belly and driving wind out of him in a gusty *whoosh*. In the same second he jerked his knife from the scabbard and whipped the blade up so that the point jabbed Larkin in the soft flesh under his chin.

"Now if you boys on the horses want a part of this play," Dolan said, "you go right ahead and pull your guns. My knife will go through his windpipe like a hot blade through tallow, and then I'll pull my gun and I'll drop both of you out of your saddles."

They had their guns half raised, but now they froze, their fear-widened eyes on Larkin. "No, señor," one of them said, and dropped his Colt back into the holster. "No fight." He said something in Spanish to the other man, who nodded and slid his gun back into leather.

Dolan laughed softly. "You take long steps, friend," he said to Larkin. "You come back in the morning. I'll be here. You try hanging me to that limb you were talking about, and I'll fill you so full of holes that they'll never find your skull. They'll just be picking up the holes."

He jabbed the point of his blade a little deeper into Larkin's flesh and brought a trickle of blood that ran down his neck. Larkin's eyes almost bugged out of his head. Sweat broke through the skin of his face and poured down his cheeks. He mumbled, "Don't . . . kill . . . me."

Dolan rose, pulling Larkin's gun as he got up. He slipped his knife back into the scabbard as he cocked the revolver. "Get up," he said. "Ride out of here and don't come back. I might even file on this spring. A man could irrigate a pretty good chunk of land with that head of water."

As Larkin stumbled to his feet and turned, Dolan took

two long steps and rammed his right foot against the man's butt. Larkin spilled forward and sprawled on his belly. He got to his hands and knees and scrambled crablike for about ten feet, then came upright and swung into the saddle. He wiped a hand under his chin and looked at the blood, then raised his eyes to Dolan.

"By God, you'll hear from me," Larkin said in a dead-flat tone. "Don't you ever doubt it."

"I'll kill you the next time you start pushing me off public domain," Dolan said, "and don't you ever doubt that."

Larkin wheeled his horse and cracked steel to him, the other two men falling in behind him. Dolan watched them until they disappeared over a ridge. Again he thought he had not hunted trouble, but it had hunted him and he had dealt with it as he always had. He'd be right here in the morning when Larkin showed up with his crew, and he had no question in his mind about Larkin bringing his crew. He'd fetch every man he could find.

Dolan built up his fire, then dug a fishline out of his pack. He cut a willow pole, hunted until he found a grasshopper, and baited the hook. He tossed it into the creek just above a deep hole. He pulled it out after it drifted into the still water and repeated the motion. On the third cast he caught a fifteen-inch cutthroat. He cleaned it and started a pot of coffee, then cooked the trout.

Twilight came slowly. After he had eaten, he stretched out in the grass beside the fire and stared at the darkening sky. He heard a coyote call from somewhere back on the mountain, then another answered. A strange, sad feeling took possession of him. Perhaps it was caused by the coyote chorus, or maybe it was an aftermath of the violence he had just experienced.

He felt the wildness that was in this land. He wished it would remain exactly as it was, but he knew it would not. He asked himself what kind of future waited for a man born out of his time. He had no answer.

Then, for no reason that he could identify, he began thinking of his schoolteacher mother and the Colorado mining camp where she had raised him, of the deep snow and the cold, and how good it had felt to come into the warm cabin after he had been sledding and smell supper cooking and hold his numb hands over the big range. His mother would pat him on the back and ask, "Have a good time, honey?"

He guessed that was the real tragedy. He had never known how good a time he'd had.

CHAPTER 2

DOLAN SLEPT LIGHTLY that night, his Winchester on the ground beside him. He thought that his visitors might come before sunup, but no one did. When it was daylight, he built a fire, caught another trout, and made coffee.

He kept his eyes on the ridge to the north, but Larkin did not appear with the F Ranch crew. No one came until mid-morning, and then his visitor was the most unlikely one Dolan could imagine.

The rider topped the ridge and came on at a good pace. He was forking a leggy chestnut built more for speed than endurance. When he came close and dismounted, Dolan saw that he was a small man, measuring five-six at the most and weighing no more than one hundred twenty-five pounds.

He was about forty, Dolan judged. He had a black moustache carefully trimmed, and his eyes were so dark they appeared to be black. He wore a brown broadcloth suit and expensive hand-tooled boots, his saddle had a good deal of silver trim, and his Stetson had set him back more than a month's pay for an ordinary cowhand. But it was plain this man was no ordinary cowhand.

Dolan's visitor sized him up as he approached just as Dolan was sizing him up. When he was a few feet away, he extended his hand. "I'm Bronc Farrel," he said. "I own F Ranch. Pete Larkin is my foreman, but he doesn't always handle things the way I like to see them handled. From what I hear, he made a horse's ass out of himself yesterday."

Dolan shook hands, admitting grudgingly to himself that he liked this man, that he was one of the friendly cowmen Dolan was inclined to forget about. He remembered the ones like Pete Larkin.

"I guess he did," Dolan said. "Why do you have a man like that rodding your outfit?"

"You just asked an interesting question." Farrel fished a cigar out of his pocket and handed it to Dolan, then produced one for himself. He picked up a burning twig from the fire and lighted the cigar, then walked to a windfall cottonwood and sat down on the trunk.

"As a matter of fact," Farrel said, "there are several reasons. Number One: Pete came north with me from California ten years ago. He has always been a good foreman. That is, he knows cattle and the buckaroos respect him and work for him.

"He managed to get almost all of my cows and bulls up here, and that wasn't an easy job because we drove through country that no one had ever driven through before. It was the first herd that showed up here in this corner of Oregon. Well, I owe a man like that something. It would be the worst kind of ingratitude if I fired him after all he's done for me and F Ranch. We even fought through the Paiute-Bannock War together."

Farrel fingered the ash off his cigar and stared at the red coal. "Number Two reason. In most cases, Pete's tough ways works. I'm not obeying the law, if there is any law that applies to a new country like this. I'm claiming land that is part of the public domain and I'm the first to admit it. I got here with about twenty-five hundred head. I built the first ranch on the west side of Steens Mountain. Today I'm worth a quarter of a million dollars, maybe more, and I didn't have anything but debts when I started north ten years ago."

Farrel put the cigar back between his teeth and tongued it to one side of his mouth. "I'm not trying to brag to you, Dolan. I don't need to brag to anybody. I'm always suspicious of a man who brags because he's trying to impress somebody, and if he's really got what it takes, he doesn't need to. I just want to tell you what has happened and what will keep on happening. I don't let people settle on any part of what I claim as F Ranch range."

Actually he was very little different from other cowmen Dolan had known. He was simply more honest, Dolan thought, in admitting he was breaking the law, but he was just as greedy and ambitious as any of them.

Farrel paused, his eyes narrowed as he stared thoughtfully at the sage flat to the west. He went on, "In this regard

Pete has done very well because he runs settlers off my range. Most settlers are easy to bluff. They don't defy him the way you did. Pete will do anything he needs to, including murder, to move them. He threatened to hang you. He'd have done it if he could, but I saw no point in getting a bunch of men killed, so I came today to talk to you. I gave Pete something else to do." Farrel laughed softly. "He didn't like it a little bit."

Farrel took his cigar out of his mouth again. Dolan was entranced by the rancher. He had never seen anyone like him. He was small, but somehow he gave the impression of being ten feet tall. Small or big, Bronc Farrel was a formidable man. Not in the bulldozing way Pete Larkin was, but more like a fox. He made his brain work instead of his muscles, and so in the long run, he would be a far tougher enemy than Larkin.

"Well," Farrel said, "to get on with my story. I carved out for myself a piece of range land and I've held it for ten years and I'll go on holding it as long as I can. I own ten sections of land, swampland I bought from the state of Oregon. The rest of my range I hold by strength without the slightest legal right. Someday a government agent will come in and force me to give it up, but until that day comes, I'll go on using it."

Farrel swung an arm toward the sage flat. "You told Larkin you might settle here and that a man could irrigate a nice chunk of land from Antelope Spring." He motioned upstream toward the spring. "That's exactly right except that I would never permit it. I judge there are more than ten thousand acres I could put under the ditch. In time that's exactly what I'll do, but right now I've got all I can do north of here, so the development of this part of the country will have to wait. I don't know how long, maybe two, three years."

He rose and tossed his half-smoked cigar into the fire. He said, "I've run on till I'm out of breath. Now tell me about yourself."

Dolan was surprised. "Why?"

"I've got my reasons," Farrel said. "I had a hunch when Larkin started telling me about running into you. Now that I'm here, and I've had a chance to see you and talk to you,

I know my hunch is right. Go ahead. Tell me about yourself."

"Nothing much to tell," Dolan said. "My father died when I was small. My mother was a schoolteacher at Black Hawk. That's a mining camp in Colorado. She taught me to read and write and to enjoy some of the old classics, though I haven't had a book in my hands for years. She died when I was twelve and I've been drifting around ever since."

Farrel nodded. "Go on. There's more to tell. I don't know what it is, but there's more to tell."

Dolan shook his head. "No, nothing more except that I've been all over the Rockies from Colorado to Montana. I've made my living trapping or guiding and scouting for the army against the Sioux. I've wintered with the Indians more than once. Shoshoni mostly. I came to Oregon for the first time last fall and went on out to the coast, but that's too damp and cold for me. This is the kind of country I like, so I came back here. The only other time I ever saw Steens Mountain was from the east side. Looks a lot different than from here."

"Good," Farrel said approvingly. "Good. I'll add one more thing. Tell me if it's true. You like to live by yourself and you have never met a woman you want to marry because you don't want to settle down and raise a family, so you keep drifting. Or maybe it's because you don't like living with a lot of people and being hemmed in by them. I'm guessing, but I've got some of those same feelings. I'm married, but, by God, I don't know why. Now I've got her and I'm stuck with her."

Dolan laughed in spite of himself. "You're dead right about the way I feel. If I ever did get married, I guess I'd feel the way you do, so I don't take the chance."

Farrel nodded. "I think we understand each other and I consider that important. I don't want to fight you and I don't believe you'd ever settle down enough to develop a farm here and irrigate this land. As a matter of fact, I doubt that you favor hard work."

Dolan laughed again. "You're dead right on that, too. I hate to make a fence or plow a field or cut wood. I guess that's part of the reason I live the way I do."

"Now that we've cleared away the underbrush," Farrel said, "I'll get at the reason I came here to see you this morning. I'll also tell you the third reason I don't fire Pete Larkin. Good help is hard to get. My buckaroos do their work, but when it comes to getting fighting men—and I've got to have fighting men if I'm going to hold what I've got—it's almost impossible to find them. I'm offering you a job, Dolan, and don't say no until you've thought it over."

Dolan raised a hand when he heard "job," then dropped it and didn't say anything. His lips had even formed the word "no," but now they straightened out into a small grin. He guessed he'd starve before he worked, but he did need a little money and he was broke. He'd see what the job was. If he could force himself to hold down a job for a month, he'd have enough to buy the few necessities he'd need for the next year.

"What is the job?"

"I'm glad you're at least willing to listen," Farrel said. "I'll tell you first what it isn't. No fence making, no plowing, and no wood cutting."

"Sounds good so far."

"I have a wire fence that runs east and west along the north side of F Ranch," Farrel said. "It's to keep settlers off my range to the south. They have a legal right to settle on it, but I don't propose to let them, so the fence stops them.

"I keep a crew of riders checking the fence every day. Their job is to see that no one comes through who doesn't have my permission. If some sodbusters cut the fence and do come through, my men run them back. They have to fix the fence if it's been cut. That's the only actual work you'd ever have to do."

"Pay?"

"Fifty dollars a month and found. There's a tent kitchen near the gate. I keep a cook there who'll fix your meals. I have several men riding the fence now, but I need more. July and August are the months when the sodbusters roll in like locusts. You'll have to sleep on the ground, but that's the way you've been sleeping most of your life, isn't it?"

Dolan fought an impulse to laugh. It was ridiculous for a man like Bronc Farrel to offer him a job holding off the homesteaders. He reminded himself that he hated cowmen, so to work for one of them, helping keep out settlers who, by Farrel's own admission, had a right to settle on F Ranch range, would be the height of folly. Or would it? There was a crazy irony about this whole business that intrigued him. It might be that he'd find a way to hit at Farrel by taking the job, and in that way he would be hitting at all cowmen.

"I'll think it over," Dolan said, "but I won't promise how long I'll stay. There's something else you'd better know. I'm not like your cowboys. I don't have the kind of loyalty they have. I've seen it, but I don't understand it."

"I don't, either," Farrel admitted, "and yet I have it from Pete Larkin and my crew. All right, think it over. Ride by tomorrow and stay for dinner. I don't want you tangling with Larkin again. He'll be gone with the crew tomorrow."

Farrel got up from the tree trunk, walked to his horse, mounted, and rode away without even a backward glance. Dolan watched him until he disappeared over the ridge, then he turned to the fire. He had not smoked the cigar Farrel had given him. Now he lighted it and puffed with relish. Cigars were luxuries he couldn't afford.

He'd take Farrel up on his offer. He knew it without thinking about it anymore. He'd work one month and put the fifty dollars in his pocket and ride away. Maybe he'd head north into the Blue Mountains, where he could winter.

He wasn't being honest with Farrel and this bothered him. He had always prided himself in being honest, but he wasn't so honest that he felt compelled to tell Farrel how he felt about cowmen or that he was taking the job in the hopes he could double-cross him.

Then again maybe he wouldn't do anything against Farrel's interest. He'd have to play the cards the way they were dealt. The truth was, that for the first time in his life, he had met a cowman he admired.

CHAPTER 3

BRONC FARREL felt very pleased with himself as he rode home after his talk with Rafe Dolan. He had heard Larkin's account of how he had tangled with Dolan, then he had talked to the two vaqueros who had been with Larkin and found that in general their stories had been the same.

He couldn't help smiling when he remembered how Larkin had stormed into his office and said he wanted to take the crew out to get a man, one man who had tried to cut his throat. He pointed to the bloody spot on his throat where Dolan's knife had punctured the skin, and when Farrel had asked him why Dolan hadn't cut his throat, he couldn't find any better answer than to say he guessed Dolan had lost his nerve.

Farrel said no to Larkin's request and promised that he'd see Dolan personally in the morning. Larkin left, cursing like a madman. The point that was humorous, Farrel thought, was that this was the first time in years when anyone had had the temerity to challenge Pete Larkin, and it was more than the man could bear.

Later Farrel had listened to the buckaroos, who said Dolan had never intended to cut Larkin's throat. He simply wanted to be let alone, and he aimed to make sure that Larkin knew it. He had stripped the last of Larkin's dignity from him by kicking him so hard he had sprawled on the ground again.

It was hard for Farrel to understand how one man, smaller than Larkin, had been able to so completely humiliate him the way Dolan had. But Rico, one of the buckaroos, said, "I can handle a gun. I can use a knife. I have killed men. But this one, he is a devil." Rico shook his head. "Pete is lucky he is alive."

Now that Farrel had seen and talked to Dolan, he believed Rico was right. Rafe Dolan was a devil, and Bronc Farrel could use a few devils. He had no illusions about his future. He had built a great ranch by using land that was not his, but year by year as good homestead land was taken in other parts of the country, the pressure would steadily increase on F Ranch.

Farrel knew as well as anyone that there would come a time when he'd lose most or all of the land that he didn't own, but he would hold and use it as long as he could. Between keeping a small army on the north side of his range and hiring the best lawyers that were available, he felt certain he could hang on for years, perhaps the rest of his life.

But he had to have fighting men, and this incident with Dolan proved to Farrel what he had suspected for the past year. Pete Larkin had slipped with age and easy living and security, and Farrel could not depend on a man who was slipping.

There was no way to be sure he could keep Dolan on his payroll. The man had warned him clearly enough. But Bronc Farrel had a way of securing loyalty from the men who rode or fought for him, and he had every reason to think that, once Dolan had started to work for him, he would feel he belonged, that he would give to Farrel and F Ranch the same loyalty other men did.

It tickled Farrel's vanity that he could accomplish what he had, a sort of "if you can't lick 'em, join 'em" procedure. Rafe Dolan was a man that no one could lick. Kill him, but not lick him, so Farrel had reversed the usual procedure and induced Dolan to join him.

The real danger here was that Pete Larkin would raise holy hell the minute he knew Dolan was working for F Ranch. The trick was to keep them apart. If he didn't, they'd kill each other. Or at least one would get killed, and Farrel had a hunch it would be Larkin.

He couldn't afford to lose his foreman, so what he'd have to do was to keep Larkin busy working cattle and Dolan riding fence with the other gunslingers he had hired. Farrel had always prided himself on taking chances and living dangerously, and keeping two men like Larkin and Dolan on the payroll was living very dangerously.

One of Farrel's chief assets was his good judgment of men, and he was confident that after Dolan had worked a month here and been paid, he'd stay on. When he had once made that decision, Farrel would put him in charge of the fence riders and double his salary, and then he'd have him. Once a man was bought, he was almost certain to stay bought.

The sun was nearly noon high when Farrel turned off the county road and crossed the yard to the stable. Every time he rode in this way he felt a great burst of pride as his gaze took in his buildings and corrals, well built and carefully planned.

The round barn had been built four years ago, a real accomplishment in a country where there was no pine or fir timber. He'd hunted for and found some giant junipers back in the gorges of Steens Mountain and he'd made them do.

He used the barn during the winters to break horses when it was too cold to work outdoors. He was a good hand with horses and a spread the size of F Ranch needed a great many saddle horses. Every time he looked at the round barn he told himself that there wasn't another barn in the world like it with its umbrella-type center truss and centrally supported rafters. Inside the barn he had built a sixty-foot stone corral. Sometimes he thought he should have been an architect instead of a cattle rancher.

There were other buildings, too, so many that F Ranch resembled a small town. He took pride in his two-story white house with the row of tall Lombardy poplars across the front, and in the heavy, dark furniture that he had ordered in San Francisco and had had shipped to Winnemucca and freighted north. He had done this for his young wife, Liz.

He had married Liz two years ago, an eighteen-year-old girl who was now a twenty-year-old disgruntled woman. He knew better than anyone else how great a mistake he had made, bringing her to an isolated cattle ranch as he had, but he had always been a man who could swallow his pride and live with his mistakes and not bellyache about them.

He dismounted in front of the stable and gave the reins to Scooter, his Paiute chore boy. The kid was a good worker for an Indian kid. He was the son of a chief who had a small band of Paiutes that were camped for the summer in Big Indian Gorge on Steens Mountain. Hiring Scooter had been a sort of insurance against the Indians raiding his horses. So far it had worked, although Pete Larkin, who hated the Paiutes, had disagreed violently with Farrel when he had given Scooter a job.

Farrel crossed the dusty yard to the stone building that was his office. At first he had used a room in the house for his office, but after bringing Liz here, he decided it was better to do his paper work somewhere else.

When he had built the round barn, he'd had a good deal of stone left over after finishing the corral, so when he cast around for material, he decided that the building might as well be constructed of stone as anything.

It could, if there was any Indian trouble, be used as a fort, but so far there had not been any such trouble after the Paiute-Bannock War. He had built a fireplace on one side of the single room, and he was glad he had because he had fled from the house on a number of cold mornings to escape the sharp edge of Liz's tongue.

On those mornings he had built a fire in the fireplace to warm the room enough to stay in it. He would build no fire today. On the contrary, the morning was warm and interior of the stone building was cool, two facts that made him thankful he had thought of using the stone.

He sat down at his desk and opened a ledger, but he had no more than dipped his pen when he heard Liz ringing the dinner bell. For a moment he sat there, his eyes closed, his hands fisted, and wondered how much longer he could put up with Liz. She must have seen him ride in.

If she'd had dinner ready, she could have rung the bell before he sat down at his desk, but no, she had waited until she knew he had time to start to work. The trouble was he found himself between a rock and the hard place. If he sent her back to San Francisco, he'd have to pay alimony, and she'd break him before she was finished with him.

He put his pen down and closed the ledger, then left the building and walked to the back door of the house. He strode into the kitchen, pumped a pan of water, and washed. After he had dried on the roller towel and combed his hair, he went to the table and sat down without saying a word to Liz, who stood at the range forking steak from the pan into a platter.

Liz brought the steak to the table and poured his coffee,

then sat down across from him and began to eat. She was a good cook and Farrel was thankful for that. Before she had come, he'd had a Chinese cook who spoke the worst kind of English; Farrel had been glad to get rid of him.

In many ways Liz was an asset. She was a meticulous housekeeper, too meticulous if anything, and she was proud of her house and furniture. She was a big woman, taller than he was, her breasts rounded and firm. She was pretty, too, with gold-blond hair and blue eyes and even features.

As far as Liz's talents as a bedmate were concerned, Farrel had no criticism of her. In fact, he almost had more than he could manage, and he thought glumly that in another five years she would be more than he could manage if she didn't change. It struck him as peculiar that, although they had not got along well together for months, her appetite had not diminished in the least.

He glanced at her several times as they ate, thinking that he wasn't really sure how their trouble had started. She said he had lied to her about the ranch not being a lonely place to live, that she would have neighbors. As a matter of fact, they did. He hadn't lied to her at all. He just hadn't told her how it was, that she would have neighbors who lived on the other side of Steens Mountain a full day's ride from F Ranch.

For a time after she first came she had cried herself to sleep every night. Once they had made long ride around the north edge of the mountain to spend a few days with their neighbors. It had been at Christmas and they'd had a good time. Liz had had women to talk to for the first time in months, and she had just about talked their legs off.

A storm hit them on their way home. Liz had thought she was going to freeze to death before they reached the ranch house. She refused to go again and she wouldn't invite the neighbors here. It was an imposition, she said, to ask anyone to make a ride like that for a few days' visit.

The trouble had started then. She had made up her mind to live here alone as far as woman companionship was concerned. She wouldn't have any part of Farrel's suggestion to hire a woman to live with her, and she refused to go back to San Francisco for a visit. Instead, she insisted on living on F Ranch and finding pleasure in slashing him with her tongue, in belittling him in every way she could.

So far he had not struck back at her, vaguely hoping she would change, but she seemed to get worse with time. Now when he finished eating and rose, he looked at her again, thinking how good their marriage had been at first and how painful it was now, the air always filled with hostility.

He said, "Liz."

She looked up, giving him a contemptuous smile. "What is it, *little* man?"

She knew how sensitive he was about his size. She also knew that no one else seemed to be even aware of his short stature, that he never got involved in a fist fight, but that he was deadly with a six-gun. All of this made no difference to her, even though she was very much aware that in a country like this a man was respected for his skill with a revolver whether he could use his fists or not. Apparently the only thing she wanted to do was to hurt him.

His face turned red, but he didn't move until he had his temper under control. He said, "I hired a man today to work for me. At least I expect him to take the job. He'll stop here tomorrow noon and eat dinner with us. I thought you'd want to know so you could cook enough for three people."

She nodded, smiling. "Of course, my dear husband."

Farrel wheeled and strode out of the kitchen. He crossed the yard to the corral where Scooter had left his black gelding. He roped and saddled the animal, and rode north toward the fence, thinking he should tell the men that Dolan would join them tomorrow.

As he rode, he found that he could not get his mind off Liz. He wondered glumly what she would say tomorrow to cut him down in front of Rafe Dolan.

CHAPTER 4

RAFE DOLAN rode into the F Ranch yard a few minutes before noon and found the layout just about what he had expected. Still, he was impressed. It was a man's ranch with everything built for utility. He remembered Farrel had told him he was married, but Dolan saw no trace of a woman's touch. No grass, no flowers, no garden. Just the row of Lombardy poplars across the front of the house.

As he dismounted by the horse trough in front of the stable, he glanced at the house and noticed the white lace curtains at the windows. That, he told himself, might be a woman's touch. He doubted that Farrel or any other man would bother with curtains.

An Indian kid came out of the stable. He said, "Me take 'em. Me water and feed 'em."

"All right, Johnny," Dolan said. "Feed them good."

"Name not Johnny," the boy muttered sullenly. "Name Scooter."

"Sorry, Scooter," Dolan said.

He had noticed the corrals behind the stable as he had ridden in and now he walked to them. He had never seen anything like them before. They were made of willows packed tightly between pairs of old growth juniper posts which were set deeply into the ground and lashed together on top with strips of rawhide.

Dolan laid a hand on a post and tried to rock it, but it didn't budge. He put a hand against the willows, but there was little give here, either. A fence like this would burn, he told himself, but unless a rancher was stupid with sparks from his branding fire, there was little chance of the fence burning.

Strange how a man learns to use the material at hand, Dolan thought. If he lived near a sawmill, he'd likely use planks or slabs. If he were near a railroad, he might use wire for the larger corrals. Or if he lived near a pine or fir forest, he'd use poles or rails. None of these materials were close, but willows were, so Farrel had built willow corrals that would last a century.

Dolan was suddenly aware that someone had come up behind him. He turned to see Farrel watching him, smiling slightly. "Ever see a stockade corral before?" Farrel asked.

"Never did."

"They're stout," Farrel said, "and as cheap as any a man can build in this country. Cut the willows green and pack them as tight as you can, and you've got a corral that will last and give you a windbreak to boot."

Farrel motioned toward the hay meadows that ran for miles on both sides of the creek. "The willows came from down there. You wouldn't know it now, but that was a swamp ten years ago. It'd mire a snipe any time of the year."

Dolan moved around the fence so he could get a better view. The grass was higher than a man's knees, the heads moving in waves as the breeze struck them. The grass would be ready to cut in a few days. The creek wound through the meadows in great sweeping meanders, with here and there spots of reeds and cattails that probably looked exactly as the whole valley must have looked at one time.

Farrel was watching him. When he turned to look at the rancher, it struck Dolan that he had never seen as much pride in a man's eyes as he saw in Farrel's dark eyes now. "You've done one hell of a lot of work in the ten years you've been here," Dolan said.

Farrel nodded, pleased. "If you'd seen it then, you wouldn't know it was the same country. It has been a lot of work. I own the land where my buildings are. The hay meadows, too, but if I wasn't using thousands of acres of public domain to run my stock on, I wouldn't have the ranch I have now. Do you blame me for hanging on to what I've got?"

"No," Dolan admitted, "but if I was a homesteader and I knew what it was like down there at Antelope Spring, I'd give you some trouble."

"I believe you would, but you're not a homesteader," Farrel said roughly, "and the ones who are don't know about Antelope Spring. They can settle in Horn Valley, those who are looking for a place." He motioned toward the north. "Lots of vacant land there, and water coming down from the Blue Mountains. Not as good land as that down south by Antelope Spring, and it will take more work to put water on it, but it's there and nobody's claiming it. I developed this spread, and by God, I'll keep it." He jerked his head toward the house. "Let's go put the feed bag on."

Dolan strode beside Farrel to the house, knowing how the man felt, but the fact remained that he was using land that did not belong to him, land that any settler had a right to claim and farm if he could get there to claim it.

Dolan would never be a farmer, but there were plenty of farmers who had families and were willing to work hard, and Antelope Spring was a natural place for such a man to settle. In a way Farrel was acting the part of a dog in the manger. As he had said, there was still work to be done here, and it would be several years before he could develop the Antelope Spring country.

It wasn't any of his business, Dolan told himself. He'd work the month and draw his wages and drift on. He didn't know where he'd go, but there were still places in the West where a man could live off the country by his own efforts. It would take some hunting, but he could find such a place.

Still, the very thing Farrel was doing was the kind of overbearing and domineering trick that always made him furious when he thought about ranchers who made their own laws and took everything they could hold by force. Before the month was over, he thought, he might be cutting the fence himself just to let some homesteaders through.

He followed Farrel into the kitchen. A tall woman was standing at the stove. She turned when Farrel said, "Liz, I want you to meet Rafe Dolan. Dolan, this is my wife, Liz."

She said, "I'm pleased to meet you, Mr. Dolan," and then stood looking at him, her eyes as aggressive as a man's would be when he is meeting a beautiful woman for the first time.

Her studied appraisal made him uneasy. He said, "Howdy, Mrs. Farrel."

She continued to look at him in her confident way for a long moment, then turned slowly to the stove. For the first time in years Dolan found himself stirred by the sight of a white woman, and he glanced at Farrel, wondering if the rancher knew what was happening. Apparently he didn't because he had started to pump a pan of water. Dolan sensed this was not a healthy situation and he wasn't sure he could work here for a month.

When Farrel finished washing, he motioned for Dolan to step up to the pump. Dolan obeyed, and when he was finished, Farrel was already seated at the table. He said, "Have a chair, Dolan. Looks like Liz has it about ready."

Dolan crossed to the table and sat down across from Farrel. Liz poured the coffee and took the chair at Dolan's right. A platter of steak was on the table along with a dish of gravy. In addition, there were beans, potatoes, hot biscuits, and honey.

"I don't suppose you're used to meals like this," Farrel said.

Dolan shook his head. "You're right, I'm not. I guess you'd starve on the prairie fare I live on."

They ate in silence for a time, then Farrel said, "You told me you'd been scouting for the army against the Sioux. I suppose you've met most of the famous scouts and guides."

"Not many," Dolan said. "Most of the great ones are gone. I never saw Kit Carson. I met Jim Bridger once. The only famous one I know pretty well is Buffalo Bill Cody, and in my opinion, his fame is greater than his talent."

"I've wondered about that," Farrel said.

"Funny thing about fame," Dolan went on thoughtfully. "Some men have a flare for getting it. Cody has. Seems to me that men like him get hold of some Eastern reporter who writes an article about him and another reporter reads it and looks the man up and writes a second article, and it begins to snowball. All the time there are a dozen other men more capable than he is who never get into the newspapers."

"For instance?" Farrel asked.

"Joel Kendall's the first one I think of. I wintered one year with him on the Popo Agie. I was just a kid then and I reckon he taught me about everything I know. Little Bat Garnier is another. Then there's Baptiste Pourier. They call him Big Bat. I guess Frank Grouard is about the best of the bunch. A lot of them are half-breeds, but they're first-class scouts and they know the country like you know your range."

"There's another thing along this line I've wondered about," Farrel said, "and that's how geography affects a man's fame. Men who fought the Sioux, for instance, are written about all the time. Generals like Crook and Miles get publicity, but out here we fought the Bannocks and Paiutes and nobody got any fame or publicity out of it."

"That's right," Dolan agreed. "It's not fair, is it?"

Liz rose, her scornful eyes on Farrel. "You got over-looked, didn't you, honey? Now that's too bad. You should have had a reporter with you when you helped chase the Paiutes and Bannocks out of Horn Valley."

She walked to the stove, picked up the coffeepot, and filled the cups, a breast pressed against Dolan's shoulder as she bent over him to pour his coffee. After that the meal was finished in silence, no one saying a word even when she brought thick slabs of dried apple pie from the pantry.

When they finished eating and rose, Dolan said, "Thank you for a good meal, Mrs. Farrel."

She smiled as if she were caressing him. "You certainly are most welcome, Mr. Dolan. I'll see you again before long."

Dolan walked out of the kitchen behind Farrel, thinking that if he stayed on F Ranch, the woman would find a way of seeing him. She would like nothing better than to stir up trouble between her husband and another man. She was a wanton, if he judged her correctly, and worse. She was a dangerous woman who would do all she could to have blood shed over her.

He glanced at Farrel as he moved up to walk beside him. The rancher's face was hard set, his lips squeezed together in a hard line. He knew, Dolan thought, and he was furious. Well, it was his business. Dolan told himself he was sure of one thing. He wanted no part of Liz Farrel.

When they reached the corral that held Dolan's horses, Farrel asked, "What have you decided? You haven't told me whether you wanted the job I offered you or not."

"I'll try it for a month," Dolan said.

"If you work a month, you'll work longer," Farrel said. "Ride north on the road. You'll come to a gate in the fence. You'll see a tent kitchen and a little tent that Whooper Bill Munk uses. He's the one to talk to. He's an old buckaroo who came up the trail with me from California, but he's so bunged up he can't ride much. That's why I gave him the job of watching the gate. He runs the fence riders. He'll tell you where and when to ride, and introduce you to the others. I intended to see all of them yesterday, but Whooper Bill was the only one I found in camp."

Farrel didn't say another word until Dolan was in the saddle ready to ride out, then he blurted, "For God's sake, man, stay away from her. She'll lead you straight to hell if you don't."

"I aim to stay away from her," Dolan said.

He rode north, leading his pack horse. He climbed another low ridge that lifted into Steens Mountain to the east, but he paid little attention to the country. In spite of his decision to have nothing to do with Liz Farrel, his thoughts turned to her and he could not shake them free of her.

He knew that she was torturing Farrel, although how much was her fault and how much was his Dolan didn't know. He felt sure it would not be long until she came to him, and he wondered what he would say and do when she did.

A man could make all the high-minded resolves in the world about wanting no part of Liz Farrel, but the truth was it would be hard to keep them when she turned her sultry attention on him. It would be smart to keep riding north, but he knew he wouldn't.

CHAPTER 5

WHEN DOLAN topped the ridge and looked down into Horn Valley, he forgot all about Liz Farrel. He had heard about this valley, but he had never seen it before, and he'd had no idea it was so large. To the north the Blue Mountains, covered with pines, made a black line against the sky, but they were so far away he found it hard to distinguish between mountains and clouds.

A series of barren, brown hills formed the eastern boundary of the valley; rimrock made the western edge, but it, like the Blue Mountains, was so far away that the exact line was lost in the haze of distance.

The valley was almost level, or so it seemed from here. It was covered with sagebrush except for two large bodies of water, the nearest one very blue under the clear sky, the other murky and white-rimmed because of the alkali that crusted its edge.

The first lake emptied into the second, he thought, and the second had no outlet. A line of green ran in looping curves from the mountain to the blue lake. It marked a stream that fed the lake, Dolan guessed, and would be the source of water if the valley was ever irrigated.

He rode down the north slope of the ridge, thinking of what Farrel had said about the settlers farming Horn Valley, that no one claimed it and there was plenty of water. It was typical thinking of men like Bronc Farrel.

Horn Valley would be settled eventually when the population pressure became great enough, but right now any farmer would take Antelope Spring and the land west of it every time if he had a choice. Legally he did have that choice, but only in theory. From a practical point of view, the settler had no choice at all.

Half an hour later Dolan reached the gate in the fence.

The road had curled toward the west so that now he was three or four miles from the rocky shoulder of Steens Mountain where the fence started. It ran across the southern edge of Horn Valley, due east and west, so straight that it must have been lined out by a compass, Dolan guessed.

He also guessed that few F Ranch cows ever drifted as far north as the fence. Farrel had built it to protect his holdings from the settlers. He didn't care whether his cattle ever ate Horn Valley grass or not. He had better range south of the ridge.

The fence was composed of three strands of wire. The gate was made of heavy planks and secured by a chain and padlock. Any settler who had the guts to try forcing his way south would find it easier to cut the fence than to try to break down the gate.

Two tents were near the gate. One was a small tent that probably was a man's living quarters, the second was much larger and had a stovepipe sticking through the roof. This one would be the kitchen, but Dolan wasn't sure what the small one was until an old man threw the flap back and stepped outside, then Dolan remembered that Farrel had mentioned Whooper Bill Munk.

For a moment the man's faded blue eyes raked Dolan's lanky body then apparently he remembered what Farrel had told him yesterday. He asked, "You're the buckskin feller the boss hired to ride fence name o' Rafe Dolan, ain't you?"

"That's right," Dolan said.

"Well, hell," the old man said, "you might as well git down. You're here. This is where you was headed, ain't it? First I thought you was just drifting through the country and I wondered where you came from, dressed the way you are."

Dolan swung down and shook the man's hand. "I'm a no good, lazy drifter who hates to work," he said. "Maybe Farrel didn't tell you that."

"No, come to think of it, he didn't." The old man threw his head back and cackled. "He did say you was one hell of a fighter and cleaned Pete Larkin's plow for him good. Wish I could have seen it. I'm Whooper Bill Munk, in case you didn't know. I've got the key to the gate, so it's up to me to decide who goes through and who don't."

"Farrel told me about you," Dolan said.

"I'll bet he did, I'll bet he did." Whooper Bill nodded his head and cackled again, his snaggle-tooth gums showing in a wide grin. "I came up the trail with him years ago. I was a cowhand in those days, but you pile the years up on a man and what have you got? An old, worn-out buckaroo. That's what. Hell, I got rheumatiz so bad in cold weather I can't fork a horse, but I can tell you when a storm's coming every time. Bronc don't think that's important, but he gave me this job. Kind of a pension, I reckon."

Whooper Bill pulled at an ear, his gaze running down Dolan's body again. "Yes, sir, I wished I could of seen you handle Pete Larkin. He was a purty good ramrod when we first got here, but he sure is high and mighty now. Well, pull off your gear and stake your horses out. You sleep belly up with your hat over your face right out there in the sun. You'll ride at night. The other three got here first, so they ride all day and sleep all night. Toss your pack inside my tent. Might be safer."

Dolan obeyed. Whooper Bill filled a pipe and puffed on it until Dolan finished, then he asked, "Want anything to eat?" He jerked a thumb toward the tent kitchen. "I'll work on old Bucky if you are."

"I'll wait till supper," Dolan said.

"Sit down in that good rocker yonder." Whooper Bill indicated a spot of thin air near the flap of the tent. "I'll use this here swivel chair. Brought it up from California with me."

He hunkered down in front of the tent, snickering. "Yes, sir, all the comforts o' home out here, guarding this damned fence of Bronc's. Took a lot of money to build it, and it ain't gonna do him no damn good when the blue chip finally gets laid on the table."

Dolan sprawled on the ground and filled and lighted his pipe. He asked, "Why won't it?"

"You can't hold the settlers back no more'n you can hold back an ocean tide," the old man said. "Not when the law's on their side like it is here. Oh, this fence might give Bronc a few more years and mebbe that's all he figgers on, but in the long run it won't do no good. That road you've been follering is a county road. Runs all the way to the Nevada line except that it ain't had no travel much south of F Ranch except the freight outfits that fetch supplies up from Winne-

mucca to us. When a county's organized out o' this end o'
Grant county, you can bet your bottom dollar that some
wise bastard is gonna see to it that the road's opened up."

Dolan nodded. "It's a purty good bet that'll happen, all
right."

"Purty good bet?" Whooper Bill snorted. "Why, it's as
sartin as the sunrise. Trouble is Bronc won't listen to me.
He makes up his own mind, or he listens to that fornicating
Pete Larkin. I could save him some grief, but he'd rather
have grief than my advice."

Dolan turned his head to hide his grin. Whooper Bill may
have been Bronc Farrel's adviser at one time, but he wasn't
now, a fact that plainly hurt his pride.

One of the three riders came in from the east and stopped
to get a cup of coffee. According to Whooper Bill his name
was John L. Sullivan. He was a small man with cauliflower
ears and a flat nose, so Dolan guessed he had been a prize
fighter, but Dolan saw nothing in the man that reminded
him of John L. Sullivan, the great heavyweight. The cowboy
shook hands with Dolan and went to the tent kitchen for his
coffee.

Whooper Bill scowled at the little man's back until he
disappeared into the tent kitchen. "There ain't a teaspoonful
of brains amongst the three o' them," he said in a low tone.
"You'll see when the other two ride in for supper. Plug
uglies. That's all they are." He scratched the back of his neck
and added, "O' course if they had any brains they wouldn't
take this job. Now me, I wouldn't crack nary a cap to keep
anybody from coming through the fence. Not if somebody
was real anxious to fight his way through."

"Why?"

"The fence is illegal," Whooper Bill said in disgust.
"That's why. In the long run Bronc needs the law as bad as
anybody. Worse, I reckon, because he's got a lot of prop-
erty to protect, and how can you do that without law?"

"I guess he's depending on F Ranch law," Dolan said.

"Which works for right now," Whooper Bill said, "only
right now ain't gonna last forever, and Bronc's smart enough
to know that. I figger he listened to Larkin when he built
this fence and when he started thinking about right now
instead of the long run. He's a young man and he's got a
young wife. They'll have kids, I reckon. A man oughtta

think about them and that means the long run."

Whooper Bill was right, Dolan thought, except that he wasn't at all sure Bronc Farrel would ever have any children or that he wanted any. Or Liz Farrel, either, so maybe the "right now" thinking was all that Farrel was interested in.

The other two riders came in at sunset. They were large men, beetle-browed, with low foreheads and surly dispositions. Whooper Bill introduced them as Concho and Slim. If they had last names, they apparently didn't want anyone to know them. They looked enough alike to be brothers and Dolan guessed that they were. They shook hands with him and turned and walked toward the tent kitchen.

"See what I was telling you?" Whooper Bill said triumphantly. "Not a teaspoonful of brains amongst them."

Dolan nodded, thinking the old man was right. He had another thought, too. Whooper Bill had about all of John L. Sullivan, Concho, and Slim that he could stand, and he was glad Rafe Dolan had come along.

Dolan ate supper, saddled up, and mounted. Whooper Bill said, "Ride east to the end of the fence, and then come back here and ride west another three, four miles. We don't figger any sodbusters will git no farther off the road at night. When it's daylight, come in and git your breakfast. The other three will ride out in another hour or so."

The moon was full, the sky clear, so Dolan had the advantage of the moonlight while he became familiar with the country. As he rode toward the mountain, he thought about the other three riders. He had a hunch they were wanted men, hiding out in this empty, lawless land and earning fighting pay while they did it.

CHAPTER 6

WHEN DOLAN reached the eastern end of the fence, he was not surprised to find a saddle horse next to the rock shoulder just beyond the end post and to hear Liz Farrel say, "Good evening, Mr. Dolan. Will you step down, please?"

She was standing between her horse and the rock wall, so he didn't see her. For a moment he remained where he was, thinking that if he wanted to work here for a month, he'd better stay right where he was. She had been in his thoughts most of the time since he'd seen her at noon, and he had a good idea what he could do if he played his hand carefully and well.

He swung down, filled for the moment with a compelling hunger for her. He said, "I'm surprised to see you here, Mrs. Farrel."

"No you're not," she said coolly. "You knew at noon that I would be here. The only question is how you feel about me being here. I take you for a violent man, Mr. Dolan, a man without morals who takes what he wants. Am I right?"

"Not entirely," he said. "You know that I've lived with Indians a good part of my life. I'm guessing you don't know much about them. You probably think I'm a savage just as you think they are, and therefore you think I'm violent and without morals. That's not true of me or the Indians. They're about like white people, some good, some bad."

"Perhaps." She came toward him, stopping when she stood a step from him, then she raised her hands to his shoulders. "Don't think I object to you being violent and without morals. That's the way I am. I sensed in you what I need and want in a man. You saw at noon that I am not happily married."

He started to back away, but she would not have it. She

took the one short step between them and slipped her hands around his neck. She was nearly as tall as he was, and now her lips were on his, her body pressed against him. She kissed him, and for a moment he was roused and shocked by the passion of her kiss.

She drew her mouth back from his, whispering, "Now how do you feel about me being here?"

He didn't answer for a moment. He did not understand himself; he knew he could have her, but suddenly the hunger for her was gone. He didn't have to play his hand carefully and well. He didn't have to play it at all. Something that came so easily was not worth having. "Don't come again." He turned to his horse and mounted.

She caught the bridle of his horse. "Why? Are you a moral man? Did I judge you wrong?"

"No," he said. "Even a man without morals has some principles he lives by. I don't want another man's wife, and you don't really want me. You want to hurt your husband. That's all."

"You're a fool," she said angrily.

"All right, I'm a fool," he said. "Maybe you are, too. I don't want a fight with your husband over you."

She laughed scornfully. "Are you afraid of a man as little as Bronc?"

He wasn't afraid, but he wondered if she would have more respect for her husband if he told her he was. Well, that was Farrel's problem, not his. He said, "Let's just say I don't want to kill him. Does he know you're here? I should think he'd know you were gone."

"He does," she said, "but he doesn't worry. I often ride after dark. I'm safer than I would be in a city. I guess Bronc wouldn't worry about me anyhow. Nothing in the world means anything to him except F Ranch." She released her grip on the bridle and stepped back. "I'm willing to throw myself at a man once, but never twice. Next time you'll have to come to me."

"There won't be a next time," he said.

She laughed softly. "We'll see. Are you going to continue to work for Bronc, or will you be riding on tomorrow now that I've scared you?"

"You haven't scared me," he answered, "and I won't be riding on tomorrow."

"Then you'll see me again," she said.

She whirled away from him and, mounting her horse, rode off at a dangerous pace. He remained where he was until the sound of her horse's hoofs was dimmed by distance and then lost. He turned his horse and rode back toward the gate.

He thought about what had happened, wondering why the flame had burned so wildly for a moment and then had gone out. It wasn't the way he had told her, a matter of taking another man's wife. He'd appealed to women since he'd been a boy; he had possessed other men's wives and it had never worried him. He always went on the assumption that if a man couldn't keep his wife from straying, he didn't deserve a faithful wife.

Somehow it was different with Liz Farrel. She had been there for the taking. Maybe that was the explanation. He had always liked to think he had made a conquest, but there was no conquest if there was no struggle. He knew he had not behaved as the average man would, but he also knew he was not an average man.

Liz could learn a good deal from Indian women, Dolan thought, and wondered what Farrel would say if he knew what had happened tonight. But Farrel would never know. He wouldn't tell the rancher and Liz certainly wouldn't, but if Liz had had her way, she would have told Farrel and Farrel would have come gunning for him.

The following morning he wasn't so sure about Farrel not knowing. He ate breakfast. After the three fence riders left camp, Dolan smoked a pipe before he tried to sleep. Whooper Bill hunkered beside him, staring at him closely.

Finally the old man asked, "Well, was she out there last night?"

Dolan took the pipe out of his mouth, feigning puzzlement. "Who the hell are you talking about?"

"Liz Farrel, damn it," Whooper Bill snapped. "You know who I mean. She's the only female woman in fifty miles o' here except them Paiute squaws up there on the mountain and they stink so bad a man couldn't do nothing to one of 'em."

Dolan stared at the old man's lined face, then lowered his gaze to the pipe he held in his hand. "What made you think she'd be there?"

Whooper Bill swore in disgust. "She's a whore as far as I'm concerned. She's put Bronc through the wringer too many times. I've got a notion she'd like to work up a gunfight between some other man and Bronc and get Bronc killed, then she'd fall into everything Bronc's made. I figger that's the reason she married him in the first place. She sure didn't do it for love."

"You didn't answer my question," Dolan said.

"I just guessed," he said evasively.

"Or maybe you followed me," Dolan said with biting anger. "Maybe Farrel ordered you to watch me, thinking that Liz might show up."

"Now, now," Whooper Bill said soothingly. "Bronc trusts you, though I don't know why. The thing is I know Liz. It's my guess she's smelled around after every man on F Ranch and found a way to sleep with 'em. Except me, o' course, and she knows I'm too old and bunged up to do her any good."

"I don't think she's slept with every man on the ranch," Dolan said.

Suddenly he had a suspicion that Farrel wanted to trap his wife. Maybe that was the reason he had given Dolan this job, thinking that Liz would do exactly what she had. Or maybe Farrel instead of Whooper Bill had been somewhere close enough to the end of the fence to know what had happened.

Suddenly it came to Dolan that he didn't respect Bronc Farrel as much as he had thought he did. A man should be able to keep his wife without spying on her. A prickle ran down his spine when he thought about what might have happened if he had gone as far as he could have with Liz Farrel. The chances were both of them would have been killed. She didn't really know her husband, he thought.

Two mornings later Bronc Farrel rode into camp with a young buckaroo named Willie Martin. He was friendly enough to Dolan and asked if any homesteaders had showed up at the gate. If Farrel thought there was anything between Dolan and his wife, he kept his suspicions from showing.

Farrel and young Martin had their coffee and rode on, Farrel saying casually that they were going to buy Hodig's store. After they left, Whooper Bill said sourly, "That's some of Pete Larkin's work or I miss my guess."

"What do you mean?" Dolan asked.

"Why, old man Hodig can't hurt Bronc or F Ranch none," Whooper Bill said. "He's got a little store at the foot of the grade on the Stinking Water. Got a two-bit farm back o' the store. Raises hay for the sodbusters that come through and want to put their horses up overnight. He don't have much of a store. Just flour and bacon and sugar and such. Trouble is he tells folks that there's good land south o' the fence if they want to go that far and settle on it. All they've got to do, he says, is to go south by staying on the county road."

"But they can't get through the fence," Dolan said.

"That's why Hodig ain't hurting Bronc," Whooper Bill said savagely. "We turn 'em back right here, but Larkin, he keeps telling Bronc that Hodig's got to be moved out o' his store and one o' Bronc's men put in there in his place. Then there won't be anybody to tell the settlers to go through the fence. Bronc's man will say the best place to settle is right there in Horn Valley."

"You know," Dolan said, "according to you, Bronc Farrel never does anything wrong unless Larkin puts him up to it."

Whooper Bill scowled. "I figger that's about right. Bronc's a good man, but Larkin's getting to be more of a son of a bitch all the time. Trouble is Bronc could live here forever and not be in trouble with nobody if he'd just use what's his, but instead o' that, Larkin says the sky's the limit, so Bronc breaks the law claiming land that ain't his and building fence trying to hold that land. He'll bring a U.S. marshal in here sure."

Dolan didn't want to argue with Whooper Bill, but he had a hunch that it wasn't Larkin any more than Farrel who considered the sky the limit. Later in the day Farrel stopped at the camp. He was alone.

Dolan had been asleep, but he woke in time to hear Farrel say with satisfaction that Hodig had seen the light. "He took what I offered him. He didn't have much of anything on his shelves, so I'll send a wagonload of supplies to Willie."

Dolan closed his eyes. He could guess why Hodig had

seen the light. Dolan told himself again that he had been taken in by Bronc Farrel's charm, that Farrel was just a little smoother than most cowmen, but he was no better or worse than other ranchers Dolan had known. He'd work a month and take his pay and ride away.

CHAPTER 7

DOLAN WORKED one month as he had planned. Every day he expected something to happen which would bring on a fight with the other three riders. He found himself disliking them more and more until he reached the place where he couldn't stand being around them, so he always managed to eat by himself or be asleep when they rode into camp.

Whooper Bill was even worse. He had lived with them longer than Dolan had. At least once every day he would say, "I tell you there ain't a teaspoonful of brains amongst them. Plug uglies! That's what they are."

Finally, near the end of the month, he said, "I keep a double-barreled scattergun in my tent. I wish it had three barrels, one for Concho, one for Slim, and a little one loaded with birdshot for John L. Sullivan."

They ignored Dolan as if he were inferior and therefore not worthy of notice. They treated Whooper Bill almost the same, completely disregarding Farrel's instructions that they were to take their orders from him. Dolan told himself that he had never met men who were as close to being animals as these three, and he told Whooper Bill they would kill him sooner or later if he stayed here at the gate.

"Naw, they wouldn't do anything like that," Whooper Bill said as if trying to reassure himself.

"How did Farrel happen to hire men like these?" Dolan asked.

"Why, Bronc figgered homesteaders would be showing up by the hundreds when the weather turned warm, so when them three bastards rode in one day a couple of months ago looking for work, Bronc hired 'em. He thought they were tough enough to hold off an army. I got the idea from a few hints they've dropped that they're wanted for murder in Arizona. If they wasn't scared about being strung up, they wouldn't have stayed here this long. Looks to me like they figger this is a good place to hole up."

Not more than ten homesteader wagons approached the gate during the month Dolan had been here, and they turned back without making an argument out of it. Apparently Willie Martin was doing a good job at the store discouraging settlers from trying to settle south of the fence, but on the morning after Dolan's last night of riding, a man showed up who would not be turned back.

Dolan was eating breakfast, intending to go directly to F Ranch for his pay as soon as he finished, when a covered wagon rolled up to the gate. Whooper Bill moved toward it, calling, "No one is allowed to come through the gate unless he has permission from Bronc Farrel. He owns F Ranch, and he don't want people trespassing on his range."

The three fence riders had been saddling their horses. Now they started walking toward the gate, John L. Sullivan saying something to the two big men. They snickered, and Concho said, "Sure. It's been too damned dull around here lately."

Dolan finished his breakfast and set the tin plate on the ground. He got up, his gaze on the backs of the three fence riders. He had a hunch this was going to boil up into the showdown he had hoped to avoid.

Actually he relished the prospect of having a showdown. He had heard enough talk from these men about their drinking sprees and whores and innocent people that they had robbed and beaten to tie his guts into knots. If his hunch was right, this was the morning he'd work those knots out.

The man who had been driving the team stepped down from the wagon seat. He was young, but he was very tall and very thin, and he had a cough that racked his entire body. A skinny woman and a hollow-cheeked child remained on the seat. Dolan had heard about homesteader outfits that were held together by spit and baling wire, and this was just such an outfit.

Dolan moved slowly toward the gate, staying about three steps behind the fence riders. He was too far from the man and Whooper Bill to hear what they were saying. Apparently the homesteader was not willing to abide by Whooper Bill's statement that no one was allowed to go through the gate unless he had Farrel's permission.

Suddenly the settler banged an open palm against the top plank of the gate and shouted in a wild rage, "By God, you can't keep us out. This is a county road and you can't close a county road. It goes all the way to the Nevada line and we aim to travel on it. Now open up."

The three fence riders had reached Whooper Bill. John L. Sullivan said, "Bill, this man is talking tough. Open the gate and let him drive through. He needs to be showed what happens to a man who talks tough to F Ranch hands."

"I ain't gonna open that gate for him or you or nobody else," Whooper Bill said.

Concho's big right hand closed over the back of the old cowboy's neck. He squeezed his fingers together until Whooper Bill winced in pain, then he dropped his hand to his side. "Open it," he said. "We aim to show this punkin roller what happens to men who insist on their rights."

Whooper Bill cursed and gave Concho a look of pure, deadly hatred. He drew the key from his pocket and opened the padlock as the homesteader stepped back into the seat. His wife, thoroughly frightened, screamed, "Don't go through the gate, Carl. Turn around."

Dolan had moved up until he stood a step or two behind John L. Sullivan. There he waited, not considering the three-to-one odds. He was curious about what they were going to do to the skinny settler. All he knew was that it would be so bad he'd have to stop it.

The heavy gate swung open and Whooper Bill backed away from the wagon. He shot a worried glance at Dolan, then wheeled and ran toward his tent. The wagon had barely cleared the gate when Concho reached up and, grabbing the settler by an arm, tumbled him out of the seat and onto the ground. The man had let go of the lines. His wife picked them up quickly and held the team.

The settler lay motionless on the ground, stunned. Slim gripped his shoulders and hauled him to his feet. "All right, John L.," he said. "Now you've got a punching bag. Let's see if you can hit as hard as your name's sake."

Sullivan drove a fist into the man's stomach. The woman screamed, "Don't. You'll kill him. He's a sick man."

"Shut up," Concho bawled at her. "We'll get to you later."

Dolan had seen enough. Sullivan brought his fist back for another blow. Before he had time to strike the settler, Dolan caught him by the seat of the pants and the back of his shirt collar and threw him over the fence. He hit on his head in the sagebrush and flopped on over and lay motionless.

Concho bellowed an oath and drove at Dolan, his big hands outstretched, but he didn't quite reach him. Dolan kicked him in the crotch, and from the way the big man screamed in agony and bent forward, he must have felt as if both balls had been rammed up into his belly.

Dolan wheeled toward Slim, who was slow both of body and mind. He'd had ample time to draw his gun, but he fired a second too late. Dolan's right hand knocked the barrel to one side as he drew his knife with his left. He slashed Slim's shirt open from the left shoulder to his right hip, the knife drawing blood in one long scratch across Slim's chest and belly. Dolan slashed again with the knife, this time angling from the right shoulder to the left hip, again drawing blood.

Slim screamed, "You're cutting me to pieces." He dropped his gun and backed up, both hands clutching his belly as if he had to hold his guts into place.

Dolan turned to see Concho straightening up, right hand moving toward the butt of his gun. Whooper Bill said, "Don't try it, Concho. The show's over. You pull your iron and I'll blow your god-damned head off just above the shoulders."

The old man stood in front of his tent, his double-barreled shotgun in his hand. Both hammers were back, and Whooper Bill looked as if he would enjoy nothing better than to pull the triggers. Concho's hand fell away from his gun.

"Get your horses," Dolan ordered. "You're late starting to ride."

Concho moved slowly and painfully to the horses. Slim, still pressing his hands against his belly, followed. Blood was seeping through his fingers and Dolan wondered if his blade had gone deeper than he had intended. Then he thought it would be no loss if Slim died from his wounds. In reality it would be a delayed execution. Now that he thought about it, he wished he had cut deeper.

John L. Sullivan had come to enough to crawl back under the fence. Now he stood up, his hands going to his neck and feeling it gingerly as if he thought he'd find some protruding bones. When Concho and Slim rode up, Concho leading Sullivan's horse, the little man said, "Dolan, I'm gonna kill you as sure as the sun's coming up in the morning."

"Make your draw," Dolan said. "A man should never put off a thing like that."

"Don't try it," Concho said. "We can wait."

Sullivan mounted and the three men rode west along the fence. The settler was on his feet now and leaning against a wheel. His wife said, "We're going to turn back, Carl."

"I'm afraid you'll have to," Dolan told him. "I'd let you go on through if you had a chance, but the ranch is over yonder on the other side of that ridge. You'd have a dozen buckaroos after you before you went ten miles."

The settler grunted something about there being no law in this god-forsaken country. He painfully climbed back to the seat and sat there, hunched forward and coughing until bloody froth came to his lips. As she turned the wagon, the woman said, "Thank you."

Neither Dolan nor Whooper Bill moved until the wagon was back through the gate and moving north. Then Whooper Bill closed the gate and snapped the padlock and looked at Dolan as he shook his head. "Well, sir, I've seen some tough men in my time. I've seen 'em move fast and mean, but I never seen anything like the way you moved. I don't reckon a cougar could have done it any faster'n you done it."

"Thanks for getting your shotgun," Dolan said.

Whooper Bill snorted. "You didn't need it. All I done was to save Concho's life and I'm sorry I done that. If I hadn't moved in on the game, Concho would have made his draw and you'd have killed him. Ain't that right?"

"Yeah, that's just what I would have done," Dolan said, "but it might have been a mistake. If I had killed him, Farrel and Larkin would have chased me till they caught me. This way they probably won't do anything if I don't come back on F Ranch range."

"What do you figure you'll do?"

"First thing I'm going to do is to see Farrel and draw my time," Dolan said, "and then I'm coming back and I'm going to ride through your gate."

"Was I you, I'd go around the fence and not bother with the gate," Whooper Bill said. "You can make it above that rock shoulder where the fence starts. It's a purty steep climb, but you can make it."

"You think I'd miss giving those three bastards another

whack at me?" Dolan demanded. "Oh no, they can have it if they want it."

"You're a fool," Whooper Bill snapped. "You're likewise a fool for going after your money, and you're a bigger fool for coming back this way."

Dolan grinned. "Maybe I am. Anyhow, I'll leave my pack horse here and I'll be by for him in four, five hours." He started toward his saddle horse, then stopped and turned. "I might come back to F Ranch range later on. There's something about it that's downright inviting."

"Yeah, inviting to your killing," Whooper Bill said. "Once you get through that gate, you'd best keep on riding."

Dolan didn't say anything more as he saddled and mounted and rode away. He knew that what he'd like to do was a job for more than one man. If he ever ran into anybody who felt the way he did, he would be back.

CHAPTER 8

DOLAN REACHED F Ranch before noon. He dismounted and tied, noting the thin column of smoke rising from the chimney of Farrel's stone office building. He didn't need a fire now in the middle of the day, but it had probably been cool when he'd started to work. Dolan turned toward the stone building, then stopped when he heard a man in the round barn shouting in a great rage.

Dolan shrugged, thinking it was none of his business. The voice sounded like Pete Larkin's, and Dolan had no desire to tangle with the man again. All he wanted was his fifty dollars from Farrel and then he'd shake the dust of F Ranch off his feet. He took one step, then stopped as he heard the angry voice bellow, "By God, I ain't taking this off no Injun kid. I'm gonna knock your head off."

Wheeling toward the round barn, Dolan told himself he'd see what was going on, but he knew before he reached the barn that he was going to sit in on the game. He always mentally insisted that he never hunted trouble, that trouble hunted him, but a lot of the trouble he got into was like this. He couldn't pass it up.

He opened the barn door and looked in just as Larkin brought his right hand back and slapped the Paiute boy Scooter with his open palm, a hard blow that made a popping sound and sent Scooter staggering. Dolan lunged toward Larkin as Scooter recovered and tried to kick the foreman on the shin, but his kick never landed. Larkin hit him again, this time with his fist. The kid sprawled on his back in the litter on the floor.

Larkin cursed Scooter and, stepping forward, raised a booted foot and started to kick the fallen boy, but his kick didn't land, either. Dolan caught him by the shoulder and hauled him around and hit him on the jaw. Larkin staggered back, his hands clawing the air, then he fell, his head striking one of the juniper posts with a solid, thwacking sound.

Larkin lay there, almost knocked out. Dolan stood over him, waiting for him to get up, but Larkin had no intention of getting up. He raised himself on one elbow, groaned, and fell back. He said, "Go ahead, you damned savage. Scalp me. You're no better'n an Injun. Why don't you go live with 'em?"

Dolan drew his knife from the beaded scabbard on his left side and ran a finger along the razor-sharp edge of the blade. He said, "You've got some good ideas, Larkin."

"You're fired," Larkin said, still making no effort to get up. "I told Bronc he was crazy for hiring a wild man like you. I'm gonna see him. I'll make him fire you."

Dolan sighed as he slid the knife back into the scabbard. "It would be a pleasure to lift your scalp, Larkin, but maybe it's not a good idea."

He wheeled and strode out of the barn, leaving Larkin rubbing his jaw and glaring after him with feral hatred. When Dolan stepped back into the bright sunshine, he saw that Scooter had gone into the corral after his horse. He didn't stop to thank Dolan, but got aboard and went out of the yard on the run.

Dolan stared at the boy's back, wondering if trouble with the Paiutes would come out of this. He'd heard it wasn't far to Big Indian Gorge. Scooter might be back before sundown with a war party. He had no idea what the boy had done to irritate Larkin, but regardless of what it was, the foreman was a fool for hitting Scooter and inviting trouble.

The door to the stone building was open. When Dolan stepped through it, he saw that Farrel was bent over his desk, an open ledger in front of him. Dolan said, "Howdy, Farrel. I came for my time."

The rancher glanced up and frowned. "I figured on bringing your wages out to camp this evening. I always do on the last of the month. Didn't Whooper Bill tell you?"

"No," Dolan answered. "I won't be here this evening. I'm riding on."

"The hell!" Farrel stared at Dolan, anger taking possession of him. "I need you, man. I was going to double your wages and put you in charge of that fence-riding crew.

They're too tough for Whooper Bill to manage. You can't walk off and leave that good a job."

"I told you I'd try it for one month," Dolan said. "I have, and now I'm quitting. I've never been much of a hand to work anyhow."

Farrel rose, his hands trembling as he placed them palm down on his desk. "This is a riding job, Dolan. It's not like working with your hands. I wouldn't ask you to do that. You're the kind of man I need to help me build F Ranch into the spread I've dreamed about for years. I'll make you any kind of a deal you want. Just name it."

In spite of himself, Dolan felt sorry for the cattleman. Men like Pete Larkin couldn't fill the bill, and the kind of men who did were hard to find in a new country like this. Farrel didn't have much choice. Still, Rafe Dolan's loyalty was to himself, not F Ranch or Bronc Farrel.

Dolan shook his head. "I'm not the kind of man who'll do what you want done. I'm a drifter. I live off the country and when I feel like riding on some morning when I wake up, I do it."

Farrel walked around the desk, still unwilling to give up. "You haven't given it a fair trial, Dolan." He paused, then said, "I'm a man who gets what he wants. I'm not used to being turned down. I want you to work for me."

Dolan shook his head again. "No."

Farrel stared at him for a moment, then he asked, "Has Liz got anything to do with this?"

"No. The only reason I can give you besides the fact that I never work for anybody very long is that I don't like the men who work for you." He told about his fight with the three fence riders, adding, "They'd have killed that settler for no reason. They'd have raped the woman. Now if Whooper Bill don't look out, they'll kill him. They're no good, Farrel."

The rancher backed up around his desk and stood behind his swivel chair. His face turned red. In a few seconds he changed from a man who was bidding for Dolan's help to a sullen one who acted as if he had just been insulted. He asked in an icy tone, "Is that all, Dolan?"

"Not quite. I just had another go-round with Larkin, only he didn't want to fight this time." Dolan told Farrel about it, finishing with, "I don't know if you savvy Indians or not, but you had better be prepared for a raid after Scooter tells them what Larkin did to him."

Farrel wheeled and strode to his safe that was in a corner of the room. He opened it, took out a heavy, canvas bag, and set it on the desk. He counted out fifty dollars in gold and placed the coins on the corner of the desk, then returned the bag to the safe and closed the door.

"There's your money," he said in a cold, unfriendly tone. "I've got one piece of advice. Get off F Ranch range and stay off, or I'll let Larkin take the crew and hang you like he wanted to do that first evening he met you."

Dolan picked up the money, wondering why Farrel's attitude had changed so rapidly. "You might have trouble making that stick," he said. "I kind of liked it at Antelope Spring. I may come back and settle there, and I guess I'd have to follow the county road to get to it."

Farrel stood very straight, making the most of his height. His face was still red, his lips squeezed tightly together. Dolan sensed the quivering rage that possessed Farrel, but the rancher kept it under control. He said, "Don't try it. There'll be a price on your head after today if you're found on F Ranch range."

"What's the matter with you?" Dolan asked. "One minute you're as friendly as all hell, begging me to work for you, the next you're threatening to kill me."

"I can tell you what's the matter with me in a few words," Farrel said. "If you're not with me, you're against me. It's that simple. I don't want anybody around here who's against me. Now get out."

Turning, Dolan left the building, thinking that Bronc Farrel was far from the rational man he had judged him to be. He mounted, and as he rode past the white ranch house, Liz ran out and called to him. He kept on riding, not looking back at her.

CHAPTER 9

DOLAN REACHED the gate in the middle of the afternoon. The fence riders were nowhere in sight, but Whooper Bill had been expecting Dolan and was watching for him. He asked, "Had your dinner?"

"No," Dolan answered, "but I'm going to keep riding. I'll pick up something to eat at Willie Martin's store. Open the gate, will you? My three friends don't seem to be in sight, so I guess I won't wait for them to show up."

"Sure, I'll open the gate for you," Whooper Bill said, but he stood motionless, staring at Dolan as if uncertain whether he should let him go on or not. Finally he asked, "Get your wages?"

"I got them," Dolan said as he dismounted. "I asked you to open the gate."

"I heerd you," Whooper Bill said sourly, "but I've got a mind to keep you here. You're too good a man for Bronc to lose."

"He don't want me," Dolan said. "I told him I was quitting, then he got sore and told me to get out and stay out. After today I've got a price on my head if I'm found on F Ranch range. It didn't make any sense, coming from a man like Farrel, who seems pretty levelheaded. He acted like a spoiled kid. One minute he was begging me to stay, the next he was threatening to hang me."

"I knew he didn't want you to quit," Whooper Bill said. "Tell me what happened and maybe I can tell you if it made any sense or not. I've seen him in all kinds of moods, some of 'em purty damned childish. I reckon I know him better'n anybody else, and I'll admit there's times when he ain't levelheaded at all."

Dolan told him about his trouble with Larkin and his conversation with Farrel, and added, "Larkin was a fool for doing anything that might bring the Indians down on them, and Farrel should of known better than to hire an Indian boy, with Larkin hating them like he does."

"They're Paiutes, not Sioux," Whooper Bill said.

"Sure, I've heard that a dozen times," Dolan said hotly, "but they're Indians, and it's easy to make an enemy out of any Indian. The surest way to get yourself killed by one of them is to underestimate him."

"I figger they can take care of that band of Injuns," Whooper Bill said. "Now I'll tell you why Bronc changed so fast. Two reasons. First, what he said about you being for him or against him is right. He don't want nobody around who ain't for him all the way. Two, you told him you didn't like some of the men he had working for him. You don't ever criticize Bronc Farrel. When you said you didn't like the men he hired, you were criticizing him for hiring them."

"Oh hell," Dolan said in disgust. "Does he think he's God?"

"As far as this range is concerned, he is," Whooper Bill said. "If our plug ugly friends had murdered the settler and raped his wife, Bronc would have overlooked it and said they shouldn't have come through the gate."

Dolan wondered why he had ever thought he respected or admired Bronc Farrel. It was a question he had asked himself a good many times. The man had fooled him and that was a fact. "I'll get my pack horse," Dolan said. "I'm glad to be riding north. I've had a bellyful of F Ranch and Bronc Farrel."

"He ain't the man he used to be," Whooper Bill said as he unlocked the gate and swung it open. "I figger that damned Liz has had a lot to do with it. He used to figger he was a good man, but she's fixed it so he don't believe in himself no more."

When Dolan returned to the gate leading his pack animal, he leaned down from the saddle and offered his hand. Whooper Bill shook it, saying, "I hate to see you go, Rafe."

"Maybe I'll come back someday," Dolan said. "Seems real fine there at Antelope Spring. I guess I just don't like being told I can't do something I know I've got a right to do, so I might settle there."

"Don't do it," Whooper Bill warned. "Not unless you've

got an army with you. He'll do just what he said he would. He'll turn Larkin and the crew loose on you."

"We'll see," Dolan said, and rode through the gate.

He reached Willie Martin's store late in the afternoon, dismounted, and tied in front. The building was an unpainted frame structure that was not more than a year or two old. Whooper Bill had told him about old man Hodig, who had put up the building and started the store. He had settled north of the fence, thinking that would remove him from any pressure Farrel would put on him, but he didn't anticipate Farrel wanting to control his store.

Apparently Hodig had intended to do some ranching along with his storekeeping, or perhaps put settlers up as they drove through the country. He had irrigated a meadow south of the buildings. Now it was a bright emerald in a gray setting. The grass was almost ready to cut, but Willie Martin was a buckaroo, not a farmer, and Dolan guessed he would let the hay go to waste.

Dolan went in, nodding at Martin, who came into the store portion of the building from the saloon. "Howdy, Martin," Dolan said. "How do you like storekeeping?"

"I don't," Martin said sullenly, "I'd rather make my living buckarooing any day." He stared at Dolan a moment, then said, "Say, you're that buckskin fellow Bronc hired to ride fence."

Dolan nodded. "I quit today." He dropped a gold coin on the counter. "Give me some cheese, crackers, and a can of peaches."

Martin laid the purchases and Dolan's change on the two unplaned boards that made up the counter. "What are you going to do now?"

"I figured I'd stay here tonight," Dolan answered. "Tomorrow I'll ride on. Too many people around here to suit me. I'll find me a place where there's not so many."

Martin scowled as he watched Dolan eat the cheese and crackers. He was a young man, thick-shouldered, with arms like a blacksmith's. According to Whooper Bill, he could whip anyone on F Ranch, and that was probably the reason Farrel had sent him here.

"I've got a notion to go with you and let the store go to hell," Martin said. "I'm supposed to sell folks all they want unless they're bound to go through the fence. If I find out

that's what they're planning to do, I'm not to sell 'em anything. If they don't see the light by that time, I'm supposed
to beat hell out of 'em. It ain't the kind of a job I cotton to."

Dolan opened the can of peaches with his knife and
speared a half. He ate it, savoring the sweetness and the
juicy pulp of the fruit after eating the dry crackers and
cheese. "Had many settlers stop here?" Dolan asked.

"A lot of 'em," Martin said grimly. "There'll be more
before the summer's over."

"How many have you had to beat up?"

"None. They take my word for it that Horn Valley is the
place to settle. I head 'em toward the new town that Hodig
started north of the lakes. Horn City, he calls it. He started
another store and by fall he might have a town the way the
punkin rollers are moving in."

Dolan stood in the doorway after he finished his peaches
and stared north toward the Blue Mountains. He was still a
long ways from them, the dark bulge of the pine-covered
ridges barely visible through the smoky haze.

He filled and lighted his pipe as he absentmindedly
watched a dust devil dance through the sagebrush and dis-
appear in the distance. He wondered if Hodig could supply
the settlers until they had their farms producing a living for
them. The chances were he couldn't, which meant that some
of them would be starving before the first year was out.

"I'll put my horses in your corral," Dolan said. "Got any
hay?"

"There's a little left," Martin said. "I'll have to charge
you two bits for it. Feed them yourself."

"I reckon I can do that," Dolan said. "Looks like your
hay crop's about ready to cut."

Martin snorted. "If Bronc wants that hay cut, he'd better
send a crew to do it."

Dolan led his horses to the trough and let them drink,
thinking that Hodig probably hated Farrel enough to fight
him, but he was one man and an old one at that. As Dolan
stripped gear from his saddle horse, he wondered how far
Farrel and young Martin had gone to persuade Hodig to
sell out. If he stayed in the valley, he'd find out.

He forked enough hay for the horses from a nearly de-
pleted stack, then walked back to the store. For the first
time in his life he had found a place where he'd like to live.

Maybe it was because he felt a growing urge to cut Bronc
Farrel down to size.

Stopping in the shade of the porch, he knocked his pipe
out against a corner post. He didn't understand his own
feelings. It was the lack of law here that made F Ranch
possible and usually Rafe Dolan hated law and lawmen.
Now he felt an almost overpowering urge to stay right here
in Horn Valley and give the law a hand.

He thought about it as he filled his pipe again, turning it
over in his mind, and suddenly he knew at least one reason
for him feeling the way he did. Bronc Farrel had warned
him not to return to F Ranch range. He wasn't a man who
could overlook such a challenge. He knew he was not leaving the country, not until he had established his right to
travel the county road and settle at Antelope Spring if he
wanted to.

CHAPTER 10

JOEL KENDALL rode fifty yards ahead of the Kendall wagons, a gaunt, white-haired giant of a man who sat his saddle as if he had been molded to it. He reined up when he reached the top of Juniper Summit and sat motionless, staring down at Horn Valley below him.

For a time he heard nothing, not even the slow, grinding approach of the wagons behind him; he saw nothing except the sage-covered floor of the valley that stretched for miles to the distant rimrock. He was still there when the lead wagon pulled up beside him.

His son, Lon, who had been driving, called, "How far is it yet, Pa?"

Startled, Joel turned his head to look at Lon. He had been in a distant land, the dreamland of the future. He was an old man, but he wasn't ready to die. He had a ranch to build out of the wilderness; he had made up his mind he would leave something besides money to Lon and Lon's children.

For a little while he had felt a heart-warming sense of accomplishment. He had led his family from Nebraska to eastern Oregon, a very long journey. Now they were here, alive and healthy, their destination one day's travel to the south. They would settle at Antelope Spring on the west slope of Steens Mountain.

He turned to look at Lon, the spell broken. He asked, "What did you say?"

"How far is it yet?" Lon repeated.

Joel held his answer for a moment, looking at Lon's wife, Ruth, then brought his gaze back to Lon. Funny thing, he thought. The rich, red Kendall blood had turned to water in Lon. Joel had not been sure whether it was a matter of birth, or whether it was due to repeated transfusions of fear from Ruth. Joel had never known a woman who could think up as many things to fret about as she did.

"There's a store at the foot of the grade," Joel answered. "We'll camp there tonight. Antelope Spring is another day from there."

"Pa, do you think there'll be any rattlesnakes down there?" Ruth asked.

That was exactly like her, Joel thought. Next she'd ask about Indians, then about outlaws. There was trouble ahead, all right, but not from rattlesnakes or Indians or outlaws. He felt guilty because he hadn't told the family about the trouble. He'd have to tonight; he couldn't put it off any longer.

"I don't think so," he said. "They won't bother you if there are. They'll likely stay up in the rocks."

The other two wagons had pulled in behind Lon's and stopped. They were driven by Lon's daughter, Sandy, who was twenty, and his son, Bud, who was eighteen. They stepped down from their wagons and moved forward to get a better view of the valley. Joel smiled with pride when he looked at his grandchildren. They had their share of Kendall gumption.

Bud rubbed his backside. "We'd better get there purty soon, Grandpa. My saddle sores are getting worse."

Sandy didn't say a word. She just stood and looked, perhaps shocked by the size of the valley. She was a strong, brown-haired girl who stood tall and straight, with firm, full breasts and blue eyes that could meet another person's gaze squarely. She was a competent young woman who lacked the subterfuge, the coyness and duplicity, that he had found in so many women.

Joel had learned to love and respect her on the long journey from Nebraska. He wasn't sure why, because he had little use for women in general, but it may have been because Sandy had the characteristics he respected in either a man or a woman, and at the same time she lacked the characteristics he despised.

"What do you think, Sandy?" Joel asked.

"It's a beautiful sight, Grandpa," she answered. "Look at that mountain, white-haired clear into June."

Joel laughed. "She'll be white-haired most of the summer, they tell me. Fact is, I guess the snow never goes off in some places. That's Steens Mountain you're looking at. We'll be right at the foot of it when we get to Antelope Spring." He looked at Lon. "I'll go on down to the store and see about camping there tonight."

He touched his roan gelding with his spurs and started down the long grade, the road following the ridge above the Stinking Water. He would have to buy some supplies from the store. He had seen to it that there were plenty of guns and shells in the wagon Lon drove. Too, there was $10,000 in gold in the same wagon, enough to stock a cattle ranch. It was all he had after buying the wagons and horses and supplies in Omaha. It had to be enough, he told himself. He couldn't make another fortune at his age.

All the way west from Omaha Joel had been buoyed up by the prospect of a new start for Lon. He was fifty. This would probably be his last chance, too. A few men made it after fifty, but Lon wasn't that kind of man.

Now, for some reason which he could not identify, Joel felt doubt blot out the sense of achievement that had been in him a few minutes before. He was ashamed, but the doubt was there. He should have let Lon and Ruth alone on their Nebraska farm. . . .

But a man can't go back. That had been one of the basic rules of his life. You can only go forward. The farm Lon had homesteaded and proved up on had been sold. There was nothing to go back to in Nebraska. It was that simple.

Years ago when Lon was a boy Joel had left home in Missouri and had gone to California to get rich in the gold mines. He made it and sent money home to his wife. From California he drifted north to Oregon, then to Montana and from Montana to Wyoming.

He always saw to it that his wife and Lon had enough to live on. He wrote to them and they wrote to him, although he was on the move so much the letters often took weeks to catch up with him. He intended to go home, but he never got around to it until Lon sent word that his mother had died. Then Joel did go home.

He wondered if it was his fault that Lon had turned out the way he had. He thought about it a great deal after he got back. He was too late for the funeral, of course, and he was too late to have any influence on Lon.

Joel had been gone for more than twenty years. He had expected to see a young man with energy and courage and ambition, but he found that Lon was smaller than average, he was in poor health with a nervous stomach, and with very little energy and less ambition. He seemed quite satisfied to spend his life trying to grub out a living on the same hardscrabble farm that Joel had given up on years before.

He didn't stay home with Lon, partly because he couldn't stand Ruth and partly because even at his age he refused to accept the responsibility of a family. So he drifted again, never fully free from the feeling of guilt through the following years. He couldn't keep from thinking that if he had stayed home in the first place, Lon might have grown up into a better man than he was.

He put it out of his mind. When they reached Antelope Spring they would throw the old book away and start a new one. Maybe Lon and Ruth wouldn't change, but Sandy and Bud would make it go.

When he reached the store, he found that the valley floor had leveled out. He tied his roan in front, noting that others had camped here, too. An ample supply of pinewood was piled on the east side of the store building. He saw a pump and log trough at the corner, and wheel tracks in the earth that had been cleared of sagebrush.

He glanced back up the slope. The wagons weren't in sight, but he saw the dust and judged it would be another half hour at least before they rolled in. Turning, he stepped up on the porch that ran the entire width of the building and went through the doorway into the cool interior.

When his eyes became accustomed to the gloom, he discovered that no one was here. He heard voices and turned to see a door that opened into another room. Stepping through the door, he saw that he was in a barroom. The furnishings were primitive: two planks supported by beer barrels at both ends, three shelves along the wall that held a variety of bottles, and one green-topped table surrounded by four barrel chairs.

A man behind the bar said, "Howdy, friend. What'll it be?"

"Whisky," Joel answered.

The man behind the bar was big and young. He looked more like a cowhand than a storekeeper or bartender. Joel paid no attention to the man who stood on his side of the bar until the man approached, walking noiselessly in moccasins.

"It's been a long time, Joel," the man said.

Joel started to reach for his drink, then dropped his hand and wheeled to stare at this stranger who knew his name. He was dressed in dirty buckskin. He wore a sweeping black moustache and long black hair. Joel took only a moment to recognize the man although he hadn't seen him for ten years. He let out a squall. "Rafe Dolan." He pounded Dolan on the back. "How in hell did you get to be alive and here in Oregon?"

"I never died," Dolan said. "That's why I'm alive."

Joel looked at him and shook his head. He said, "By God, Rafe, it's like seeing a ghost walk in from your past. The last time I was in Deadwood I ran into old Pokey Williams. He said you'd been living on the Sweetwater and you got into trouble with a Shoshoni buck and he said this buck let you have it in the back. Pokey said you was dead and they buried you there."

"Like I said, I never died." Dolan scratched a stubble-covered cheek and added, "The way the world's been filling up with people, I don't know but what a man might as well be dead. Give me that bottle, Willie. Let's sit over yonder in one of his comfortable chairs, Joel."

"Can't do it," Joel said. "I've got my family coming down the Stinking Water." He turned to the storekeeper. "We want to camp here tonight. I've got a horse and three teams."

The storeman nodded. "Two bits a horse for hay and water. You take care of your horse yourself."

"We'll need some supplies, too," Joel said. "Ain't much between here and Boise. After supper we'll come to the store and stock up."

"Glad to have your trade," the storeman said as he held out his hand. "I'm Willie Martin."

Joel shook hands with him and turned toward the door.

He stopped when Dolan laid a hand on his arm. "You said family? You're not married. Not old, hell-raising Joel Kendall. Remember what you used to say? A wife was a millstone around a man's neck."

Joel grinned. "I was married a long time ago. She's dead. I've got a son, and he's got two kids who are about growed up. We're moving out here, lock, stock, and barrel."

"I never figured you for a married man," Dolan said.

"I'll take care of my horse," Joel said abruptly, and turned away.

He left the saloon and led his roan to the trough by the corral gate. He remembered the winter he'd spent with Dolan. They'd trapped and lived off the country, and by spring they were starving because they couldn't find much game. He'd had some tough winters in his seventy years, but that one was the toughest.

Joel finished taking care of his horse and walked slowly back toward the store, still a little shocked from running into Rafe Dolan. He had taken a liking to him as a boy and they had got along well through that hard winter, a situation designed to test what was in a man.

He guessed he had been guilty of bragging about his exploits just to impress Rafe. They had broken up in the spring, both too fiddle-footed to stay in any one place or to continue their partnership. He had not heard of Rafe since then except for the story of his being murdered on the Sweetwater.

That was the way it had always been with him, the same as knowing he couldn't go back. Forget as much of the past as you can. You can't change what's happened. All you can do is to live today, live it like a man and not wallow in fear of what may happen to you in the future.

At seventy Joel Kendall was still a good man. Then, looking at Lon, who was slumped tiredly in the seat of the lead wagon, he told himself he was a fool. He had only a few years left. He could not go on taking care of Lon in a wild country like this. He could not give Lon any of his self-reliance and independence. He could not give anything to Lon or his grandchildren except the gold in the lead wagon and that wouldn't last long, once he was dead.

Standing with his back to the sun, Joel motioned for Lon

to turn off the road to the campsite east of the store. To-night, he thought, he would have to tell them about Bronc Farrel and F Ranch and the fence that was between them and Antelope Spring.

CHAPTER 11

RAFE DOLAN filled and lighted his pipe and then, standing on the store porch, watched Joel Kendall motion the wagons into position. He saw the drivers get down and stretch, tired from the long hours in the hard seats, and was interested in how Joel kept his fingers on everything that was done.

Dolan was even more interested in the fact that one of the drivers was a young woman, tall and shapely and, at this distance, very attractive. Joel built a cook fire as the woman disappeared toward the barn with her team. Somehow she didn't fit the picture he had of white women.

He didn't remember any of the women his mother used to visit in the mining camps when he was a boy. After he started making his own living, he had not known many white women except the prostitutes in towns like Deadwood and Miles City. The few decent ones he had known were married and had too many kids. They were always tired and nervous and eternally busy wiping their children's runny noses.

This girl would be Joel's granddaughter, Dolan guessed. He saw that Joel, finished with his camp chores, was striding toward him. Taking his pipe from his mouth, he knocked it out against the nearest post. When Joel reached him, he asked, "That your granddaughter? The one driving the gray team?"

Joel nodded. "Her name's Sandy. She's the oldest of my two grandchildren. She's a fine girl." He jerked his head at the saloon. "I'll take that drink now. It'll be a spell before supper's ready."

"Good," Dolan said. "I'm always ready for a drink."

"How about eating supper with us?" Joel asked. "That is, if you can stand prairie fare."

Dolan grinned. "Glad to. What I'd eat by myself wouldn't even be good prairie fare."

"I want you to meet my family," Joel said. "Or them meet you. We ain't seen a man wearing buckskin before."

"You ain't likely to see another one, neither," Dolan grunted.

Dolan led the way into the saloon, took a bottle and two glasses from the bar, and carried them to the table. He dropped into a chair, motioning for Joel to sit down across from him. He leaned back, trying to remember how old Joel was. He wasn't sure, but he guessed about seventy, and that was very old for a man who had lived the rugged life Joel Kendall had.

Glancing at the bar, Dolan saw that Willie Martin had disappeared. Probably gone back to his living quarters to cook his supper, Dolan guessed. Dolan filled the glasses, then let his drink stand, his eyes on Joel.

"Where you headed?" he asked.

He was afraid he knew. Joel wasn't the kind of man who would bring his family out here to starve on a sagebrush farm in Horn Valley. Dolan remembered that the old man had been in this part of Oregon years ago and he very likely had seen some of the springs and streams south of F Ranch.

Joel lifted his drink and gulped it, then set the glass down. "I'll answer your question purty soon, but first I want to know what you're doing in this country."

"I've been working for F Ranch," Dolan answered. "I quit this morning. I ain't one to work no longer'n I have to, so when I had a month's wages coming, I took it and pulled my freight."

"I'm surprised you worked a month," Joel said.

"Well, I wasn't exactly working," Dolan said. "I was riding fence, keeping pilgrims like you from coming onto F Ranch range. I wouldn't have done that except I was broke and I had to have a little dinero to buy shells and tobacco and such."

"Riding fence," Joel said thoughtfully.

Dolan nodded. "That's right."

He was sure that Joel was going to ask about it, but he

didn't. Instead, he asked, "Where you headed now?"

"Anywhere I can find a place to camp," Dolan answered. "There's plenty of game in the Blue Mountains and I figger I can find it."

"Yeah, if it's there, you can find it," Joel said. "You know, Rafe, when I rode through this country years ago, there wasn't no cattle ranches, no store, no nothing, 'cept a few Paiutes and some antelopes and a hell of a lot of birds on the lakes, but I seen some purty streams and valleys south of here, and I told myself that if I ever wanted to start a cattle ranch, this was the place to come."

"That's right," Dolan said, "if you live long enough to start your spread."

Joel glanced at him sharply, then went on, "Last winter I ran into a feller in Dodge City who had settled at Antelope Spring. He put up a cabin and made some stone fence, then a bunch of F Ranch buckaroos moved in on him and told him to git. He said he wouldn't do it, so they put a rope on his neck and made out they was gonna string him up, so he changed his mind. He was still sore about it and claimed he was coming back some day and kill the F Ranch foreman. Larkin, I think his name is."

"That's right," Dolan agreed. "Pete Larkin."

"He'll never come back to do no such thing," Joel went on. "You start hanging a man and you scare the guts out of him. Anyway, he told me about the country and said it was still open and ready to be taken, so I figured this was the place to come, but now we're here, I'm a mite uneasy."

"I'll tell you something that'll make you more'n a mite uneasy," Dolan said. "It ain't just the foreman. It's the owner, Bronc Farrel. He claims Antelope Spring as part of his range, though he admits he don't have no legal right to it. You'd have to go through the fence I've been riding and fight his men to do it. Then if you did get through, you'd have to tangle with Farrel's buckaroos to hold it."

"We can do it," Joel said. "Leastwise I'm willing to try. We'll find out about the others tomorrow."

"One more thing," Dolan said. "This store belongs to Farrel. Willie Martin runs it, but he's Farrel's man. He's planted here to turn settlers into Horn Valley and tell 'em not to go south. If you tell him what you're fixing to do, he won't sell you nothing, and he'll beat hell out of you if you say you're gonna try it anyhow."

Joel snorted. "I'll tell him where we're going, and if he won't sell us what we need, we'll take it. He won't beat hell out of none of us, neither."

Dolan had his drink and set his glass down. He'd known for several minutes what he was going to do. He said, "I'll go along with you. I guess you can use another gun."

Joel grinned, relief breaking across his face. "Well now, I'm glad to hear that. We can use another gun and that's a fact. I'll pay you fifty dollars a month and beans. That fair?"

Dolan rose and held out his hand. "It's a deal. I was thinking while you were talking that this is the best chance I'll ever have to get a whack at Larkin and Farrel. They're both robbers, but it'll be a long time before the law comes in to cut 'em down to size. I don't want to wait that long."

"Funny thing," Joel said thoughtfully. "I didn't figure we'd find a place these days where there's no law except what you make."

Dolan hesitated, not sure whether he should tell Joel he was bucking odds that were mighty damn long, then decided not to. Joel knew without being told. He'd never been a man to stop because he was up against long odds, and he wouldn't stop now.

"It's the kind of place we've both been looking for," Dolan said.

"Let's go see about supper," Joel said.

As they crossed the room Dolan asked, "What'd you say your granddaughter's name was?"

"Sandy." Joel went through the door, then stopped on the porch and faced Dolan. "Well, by God, now I know why you was willing to hire on with us. I was wondering. You seen Sandy, didn't you?"

"Yeah, I seen her."

"Let me tell you something right now, Rafe," Joel said roughly. "She's going to marry a man who'll work, not a drifter wearing buckskin."

"You sure take long steps." Dolan laughed. "I ain't got around to marrying her yet, but who knows? Maybe I'll go to work. The way things are going, I'll be starved into it."

"I figure you will," Joel said. "There's talk now of a railroad coming up the Malheur. If that happens, this country will change overnight. We'll have some law in here besides Mr. Colt's."

"I know," Dolan said gloomily. "I'll either go to work or go to Canada. It's that simple."

CHAPTER 12

BUD KENDALL pulled his wagon in behind Sandy's and stepped down. He rubbed his back side and stretched and yawned. It had been a long day and he was tired and hungry. Well, tomorrow was the end of the journey and he was glad. He couldn't face more than the one day of travel.

He touched his stubble-covered cheeks and thought with disgust that his whiskers felt more like peach fuzz than honest-to-God stubble. He guessed time would take care of it. Time took care of a lot of things if a man was willing to wait for it.

Joel came by, telling him to unhook and pull off the harness and water his team, then put the horses in the corral and feed them. He strode on to Sandy's wagon to give her a hand. Bud looked at his ramrod-straight back and shook his head in admiration. Grandpa was one hell of a man.

During all his growing-up years, Bud had heard very little about his grandfather. Just that Joel Kendall was alive somewhere, that letters came now and then and usually contained money, but Bud's father never mentioned him, and his mother belittled him as a shiftless drifter if she mentioned him at all.

But they always kept the money. After they lost the farm in Missouri, they moved to Nebraska and homesteaded, and more than once the money meant another year of survival instead of losing the place as they had lost the Missouri farm.

The only thing that bothered Bud was his grandfather's failure to realize that Bud was old enough to think out some things for himself. Taking care of the team was a forinstance. All the way out here Grandpa had figured which road they'd take and where they'd camp and what supplies they'd buy. It seemed that the old man still considered Bud's father and mother as children and that was ridiculous.

Sandy finished with her team before Bud did. She waited for him outside the corral and walked back to the wagons with him. She said, "One more day to go."

Bud nodded and glanced at her as she strode along beside him in her long, black skirt. It struck him that she could do just about anything a man could. For several years she had helped with the farm work. She could do more work than her father could in any one day. That wasn't because their father was lazy. It just seemed that Lon Kendall always went through the motions, but never accomplished much.

Suddenly he asked, "Why weren't you born a boy, Sandy?"

She laughed. "Because I was born a girl, silly." Then the laughter left her and she shook her head. "Just tell me how I'll find a husband in this god-forsaken country? What are we doing out here anyway?"

He stopped. She took two more steps before she turned and faced him. "I wish I knew," he said gloomily. "Nebraska had some things wrong with it, but compared to this desert, it seemed like Paradise."

"Maybe it'll be different when we get to Antelope Spring," she said.

"It won't." He glanced back at his father, who was coming out of the corral; then he leaned forward and lowered his voice. "What do you suppose Grandpa said that persuaded Pa and Mom to sell out and come to a country like this?" He made a sweeping gesture. "Sagebrush. Juniper trees. More sagebrush. More juniper trees. That's all there is."

"Grandpa can be very persuasive when he wants to be," Sandy said. "Besides, we weren't getting anywhere back home. You've heard Pa talk about a new start."

"Yeah, I know," he muttered.

He walked on toward the wagons, Sandy falling into step with him again. He knew why they had come. He guessed he just hated to admit the truth.

For one thing, his parents had never been out of debt as long as he could remember. There had never been more than barely enough food to eat and just enough cash to buy new clothes when their old ones were literally falling apart.

A second thing was that they always seemed to be beaten out of a crop when prices were high by some devilish force of nature. Hail. Drought. Floods. Grasshoppers. Or, if they had a crop, prices were so low they couldn't make anything. Then he thought gloomily that a new start wasn't going to help. His parents would be the same people in Oregon they had been in Nebraska.

When Bud reached the wagons, he saw that Joel had started a fire and his mother was getting supper. He picked up the ax his grandfather had left beside the fire and, walking to the pile of wood next to the store and saloon building, began to split the chunks of pine.

A few minutes later Bud was aware that his grandfather had left the saloon with a stranger and was introducing him to the rest of the family. Bud straightened up and looked at the man, wondering if he was really seeing what he thought he was. The man was dressed in dirty buckskin and moccasins, he wore a revolver and a knife, and his broad-brimmed black hat was much the worse for wear.

Bud's first thought was that Buffalo Bill's Wild West Show must be in the area, but he knew that couldn't be true. There weren't enough people around here for that. The man must be real, but the time for mountain men and army scouts was long past.

Bud was still standing there staring at the man, the ax dangling in one hand, when Joel brought him to Bud. "This is the youngest," Joel said. "Best teamster in the family. Leastwise he brought his horses through in the best shape. Bud, meet Rafe Dolan."

The buckskin man held out his hand, smiling under his black moustache. "Pleased to meet you, Bud. Good teamsters is something they'll always need in a country like this." He turned to Joel. "I'll tell you one thing. You've got your work cut out for you, building a ranch out of a wilderness like this, but Bud's a big one. I reckon he can help."

Joel nodded. "We figure it'll be work. Likewise we figure on Bud helping."

"I've been thinking about us running into each other out here," Dolan said. "It wasn't no accident. We're both looking for something that maybe don't exist no more, but this corner of Oregon was as likely a place to look for it as anywhere."

"I reckon so," Joel agreed. "Trouble is, if you find what you're looking for, you ain't real sure you can take it, or hold it if you do take it."

"What do you mean by that, Grandpa?" Bud asked.

"I mean it's the same out here as anywhere else," Joel answered. "You've got to fight like hell for anything you've got." He jerked his head toward the fire. "Let's put the feed bag on, Rafe. Looks like they've about got supper ready."

Joel led the way to the fire, Bud and Dolan falling into step behind him. Dolan asked, "How do you like this country?"

"I don't like it a little bit," Bud answered. "Too much desert to suit me."

"All this land needs is water," Dolan said. "See that meadow yonder?" He motioned toward the hay field south of the store building. "Willie Martin irrigates from the creek that comes down off the Steens. That is, old man Hodig, who used to own the store, did. I guess Willie don't work at it. It'll be the same down there by Antelope Spring."

They reached the fire and helped themselves to meat and biscuits and coffee. Later, holding his tin plate in front of him as he hunkered by the fire, Dolan asked, "You all set for trouble tomorrow?"

"Trouble?" Ruth screamed the word at him. "What do you mean?"

"I ain't told 'em," Joel said uneasily. "I figured the first thing was to get 'em here. The second thing was to do whatever had to be done."

So there was going to be trouble, Bud thought. He should have guessed it. You just didn't find free land these days that was any good unless there was a reason for other settlers missing it.

He knew how big ranchers operated. They took all the land they could get under their own name and controlled the rest by one means or another, usually by sheer force and fear where there was no law enforcement. That certainly was true in this country. There probably wasn't a star-toter in a hundred miles of here.

Ruth was speechless, her thin face very pale. It was Lon who asked, "Well, Pa, what kind of trouble?"

"I ain't sure right now, but we'll find out tomorrow," Joel said. He told them about Bronc Farrel and the fence, adding, "We'll stay on the county road, so we won't be breaking the law. If Farrel's men try to keep us from going through the fence, they'll be the ones breaking the law."

No one said a word for a full minute, then Sandy said passionately, "Mr. Dolan, you are an anachronism."

The buckskin man frowned, then laughed as he dropped his plate into the wreck pan. "I don't know whether to plead guilty or not, ma'am, not knowing what that four-bit word means." He picked up the coffeepot as he pinned his gaze on Sandy. "Now suppose you tell me whether you're insulting me or not."

"You don't belong to our time," she cried. "You should have been born sixty years before you were."

"I'll plead guilty to that charge," Dolan said amiably. "Only thing is I didn't have much to do with picking the time I was born."

Joel stared at Sandy as if she were out of her mind. "What's got into you, Sandy? You're forgetting all the manners you was ever taught."

She wiped a hand across her face and shook her head. "I'm tired, Grandpa. Now that we know about this, I'm sick, too. Sick just thinking about it. You can't turn the clock back. I don't see why you're trying to."

"I don't know what you're talking about," Joel said.

"Then I'll tell you," Sandy said. "I guess there was a time when you could use a gun to get what you wanted, but that time's gone. You've got enough money to buy a good farm somewhere, but no, you bring us out here to this desert and tell us about free land, and then after you're here, you tell us about a big rancher who won't let us get to Antelope Spring. Are you going to tell us how many will be killed getting through that fence?"

"No, I won't tell you that," Joel said in a low tone. "I don't have enough money to buy a real good farm, Sandy. I figure I've got enough to get a start out here, a good start that's worth fighting for." He shot a glance at Dolan, then brought his gaze back to Sandy. "I don't think any of you folks will get killed. Rafe's going with me. We'll bust through the fence. Your job is to roll the wagons through the gate after we've opened things up."

Dolan was watching Sandy, a small smile tugging at the corners of his mouth. "I reckon this sounds purty bad to you, ma'am, but it looks to me like you're forgetting one thing. Progress don't come to all parts of the country at the same time. It's late coming here. That's why it's possible for you folks to have a fine ranch at Antelope Spring if you're willing to work and fight for it." He paused, then went on softly, "And you'll have to use your guns when you do the fighting."

He tossed his empty cup on the ground beside the fire and said, "I reckon it never occurred to you, living where you did, but it makes folks feel good to have a hand in opening up a new country. Some of us may get killed doing it, but that's the risk you always have to run."

Dolan walked away. Joel said gruffly, "Like I told you, he's going with us. He may be the one who gets killed, and all the time it's our fight. Now I'm going to order the supplies we need from Martin. We'll get loaded up tonight and be rolling by sunup. Me'n Rafe will go first. By the time you all get the wagons to the fence, we'll have it open."

The old man strode toward the store. For a moment there was no sound but the hard breathing of those who remained around the fire, then Lon said reprovingly, "Sandy."

She whirled to face her father. "I'm not sorry I said what I did. We shouldn't have come. Grandpa could have given us a new start somewhere else. Maybe not the fine farm he was talking about, but good enough."

"I say you're wrong," Bud said. "I've been thinking about what Dolan said. You know, feeling good about helping open up a new country. Well, don't forget somebody had to open up Nebraska or we couldn't have lived there. What we do tomorrow is going to help give a home to somebody else."

"That's right," Lon agreed. "What's more, we're all going to help Pa and Dolan do what fighting has to be done to get through that fence." He stopped, then said as if talking to himself more than the others, "Sometimes it's easier to die than to keep on living."

Bud looked at his father in surprise. Lon Kendall had never been one to do any fighting. Bud was surprised that he would even think about it now. Lon was staring across the desert at the Blue Mountains, almost hidden by the haze. The bright light of the dying sun was on his face. Bud, watching him, saw an expression there he had never seen before. He didn't know what it meant. Not until later.

CHAPTER 13

SANDY HELPED her mother clean up after supper, working with a kind of frenzy that wasn't like her. Nothing that Bud or her father had said had changed her mind about living out here in this wild country, or made her any more willing to accept Rafe Dolan than when she had first seen him, but she did admit to herself that she should not have said what she had to him.

As Joel had said, Dolan was going with them in the morning and he might be the one who got killed. Still, she wasn't sorry she had said it, and she certainly wasn't going to apologize to him. She had meant every word. Rafe Dolan belonged to the past and she was determined to live in the future.

When she and Bud had been small, they had often played cowboys and Indians and she usually wound up getting scalped. Their game had been about as realistic as the life Rafe Dolan was living. He was a kid, she thought bitterly, a big, overgrown kid who was pretending he was something he wasn't.

Bud dropped an armload of wood beside the fire. "Still thinking the same way, Sis?" he asked.

"The same way," she said angrily. "Seeing this man Dolan in his crazy getup is about the same as seeing one of King Arthur's knights ride out of the sagebrush. We're not living in his age, Bud."

Bud scratched his head thoughtfully. "I guess I thought the same thing when I first seen him, but I've changed my mind. I like him. He's no phony. No more'n Grandpa is. Grandpa don't wear buckskins, but thinks and acts just like Dolan."

"It's different with Grandpa," she argued. "He's an old man. He really did live in the days of the scouts and mountain men." She smiled as memories crowded into her mind. "I remember when he rode up to our house last spring. I'd never seen him before. Not that I recollect anyhow. When I looked at the gun he was carrying, and the fine horse he was riding, and the other things: the expensive boots and the Stetson and the calfskin vest—" She giggled. "I thought he was going to a party or something."

Bud nodded. "I thought the same thing, but after traveling out here with him, we found out he was a hell of a good man. I wish Pa—"

He stopped, but Sandy knew what was in his mind. He couldn't bring himself to say it plain out, but he was thinking that it was too bad their father wasn't more like Joel Kendall. She was sure that was what Bud had started to say because she'd had the same thought a dozen times every day since they left Nebraska. Lon Kendall had lived with failure as long as she could remember.

"Grandpa's old enough and he's got money enough to wear the kind of clothes he wants," Sandy said. "Besides, his duds fit the time and place, but Dolan's—"

She stopped and turned toward the store as loud, angry voices came to her. Joel and a stranger were arguing. She couldn't make out the words, but there was no doubt about the fury that gripped both men. The stranger must be the storekeeper. Martin, she thought Joel had called him.

Joel stood half a head taller than Martin, but the storekeeper was much broader in the shoulders. Sandy guessed she had never seen another man as deep-chested as this Martin. He should be using those great muscles to earn a living instead of running a store, she thought.

She turned back to Bud, remembering something she wanted to say. "You said it would be a good feeling to help open up a new country. I don't think so. Not good enough to get yourself killed for, and that's what it's going to mean to some of us. I can shoot a gun, too, and I suppose I'll have to if we go through the fence in the morning. I sure won't get a good feeling out of it, though, especially if I kill one of the others."

"That's because you're a woman. I'm a man and I don't agree with you." Bud's tone was superior as if he understood this situation which was so mysterious to a woman. "I guess women have been trying to find peaceful ways of doing things ever since Adam and Eve, but a man has to prove he's a man. That's how he gets that good feeling Dolan was talking about."

Sandy glanced at her mother, who had moved away from them to the tailgate of the lead wagon. She said, lowering her voice, "It's a feeling Pa never had, I guess. He runs around like a chicken with his head cut off. Maybe that's the real reason Grandpa insisted on coming out here. He probably thought that making a new start would change Pa."

"It won't," Bud said sourly. "I used to think that if Pa could plan a little better, we would get a living out of the farm, but I guess he just can't do it."

"Grandpa can do all the planning we need," Sandy said. "As long as he's alive, everything will work out."

"Yeah," Bud said, "which same you know won't be much longer. He's over seventy now." He turned away, adding, "I'll fetch in enough wood for breakfast."

Sandy finished picking up around the fire, thinking how much she hated this desert country, the gray sweep of land and the barren rimrock that inclosed the valley. She had not realized until tonight that she had liked the green, Nebraska plains far more than she had known when she had lived there.

Then, for some reason, she wondered why she disliked Rafe Dolan and had right from the moment her grandfather had introduced them. She had felt his gaze move slowly down her body from her head to her boots. He had liked what he had seen, she told herself ruefully. He'd made that plain enough.

For a moment his eyes had fastened on her breasts, again on her hips, and she'd had the definite impression that he had been sizing her up the way a cattle buyer sizes up a beef. Well, damn him, she told herself passionately, she was not just another squaw for him to sleep with. If he ever made out that she was, she'd cut his heart out.

A bellowed oath from the front of the store brought her around quickly. The big storekeeper, Martin, was shaking his huge fist under Joel's nose. It must have been Martin who had shouted. Rafe Dolan was standing in the porch, watching, his pipe in his mouth.

Joel began to back up, then suddenly changed his mind

and took one step forward. He swung his right in a long, looping blow that caught the surprised Martin flush on the jaw. Martin had had plenty of time to duck the punch, but apparently it was the last thing he expected an old man like Joel Kendall to do. He staggered back, tripped on the edge of the porch, and sprawled full length on the boards.

Apparently Joel thought he had knocked Martin cold. He wheeled and started toward the wagons. Martin had not been hurt seriously, for he bounced up, overtook Joel, and grabbed him by a shoulder. He whirled the old man around and drove a fist into his belly. Joel bent forward, hugging his middle as he fought for breath. Martin, seeing that he was helpless, slugged him on the chin. Joel sprawled on his back and lay motionless.

The instant Joel went down Bud started running toward the store. His mother cried, "No, Bud, no." He acted as if he hadn't heard. Dolan was bending over Joel's motionless body when Bud reached him. Martin had disappeared into the store. Dolan straightened and looked at Bud.

"He's colder'n a side of bacon," Dolan said angrily. "It sure is a hell of a note when a young buck like Martin tangles with a seventy-year-old man."

Bud lifted his feet and Dolan took his shoulders. They carried him to the lead wagon and laid him down. Bud wheeled and started back to the store. Dolan caught him before he had gone twenty feet. He said, "I'll take care of Martin. You stay here with your grandpa."

Bud stopped and stared at Dolan, his young, bony face hard set. "It's my chore," he said. "I'll attend to it."

"No," Dolan said. "Getting yourself half-killed won't help a damn bit."

Bud hesitated, then nodded and reluctantly followed Dolan back to the others. Dolan stopped when he reached Sandy. He said, "They were fighting about going through Farrel's fence. Martin is Farrel's man. I guess you knew that. Farrel put him out here to talk folks out of going south on the country road and settling down there where you're aiming to settle."

Dolan made an inclusive gesture toward the Blue Mountains to the north. "The sheriff's on the other side of that mountain range. There ain't even a deputy in these parts." He looked directly at Sandy. "I reckon it never occurred to you that there would be an area out here bigger'n some eastern states where there wouldn't be a sheriff or a deputy or a marshal."

Sandy, meeting Dolan's gaze, was suddenly aware that there was a deadly quality about the man's dark face. She saw it in his narrowed eyes, in the tight-lipped expression on his mouth, in the way his hand brushed the butt of his gun and then fell away. Joel had said Dolan had lived among the Indians. Now she shivered, wondered if she would see him scalp Martin before he was done with the storekeeper.

Dolan's eyes swept the rest of the Kendall family, then he said more slowly than before, "Joel counted on buying supplies from Martin. At first Martin was willing to sell, figuring you folks would be going on to settle on the Crooked River or the Deschutes, or maybe even right here in Horn Valley north of the fence. When Joel told him you were going south to Antelope Spring and nobody was gonna stop you, he got hostile and wouldn't sell Joel anything. They argued awhile over that, then Martin called Joel a name and that was when Joel knocked him down."

Dolan turned to Bud. "Like I said, it won't do no good for you to get half-killed or maybe killed complete, which same Martin could do. Or make an invalid out of you, which would be worse. I know how to handle him. I know how to persuade him to sell Joel those supplies, too."

Apparently he saw that Bud was only half convinced. He added, "I've got some settling to do with Bronc Farrel and the whole damned F Ranch outfit. This is where I start."

Without another word Dolan turned and strode back toward the store. Sandy stared at his straight, broad back, admitting to herself that in spite of her instinctive dislike for him, she would rather have him for a friend than an enemy.

Suddenly Sandy felt a wave of sympathy for Willie Martin.

CHAPTER 14

DOLAN HAD KNOWN what would happen. He had stood on the store porch and had heard every word that had passed between Joel and Willie Martin, and he told himself there was only one way it could end. He had no regret for not stepping in. Joel Kendall would not stand for anyone interfering in his fights. Not as long as he was still on his feet. He would feel the same way if he was ninety instead of seventy.

Dolan wondered if Sandy would understand that, or would she blame him for letting Joel take the beating that Martin had given him? From what he'd seen of her, he decided that she'd blame him. It seemed that she didn't understand anything that was happening.

When Dolan reached the store, he stopped ten feet from the porch, calling, "Martin."

Willie Martin took a good thirty seconds to move from the bar to the door. He stopped there and leaned against the casing, glaring at Dolan. Finally he said, "Well, what do you want?"

"Come on out here," Dolan said.

Again it was a good thirty seconds before Martin straightened, said defensively, "You seen the old goat hit me," and stepped across the porch and onto the ground. "You figger I was gonna stand there and let him walk away?"

"I seen it, all right," Dolan said. "Now you've got something coming and I aim to give it to you."

He hit Martin on the nose, a straight, driving right that snapped the storekeeper's head back and smashed his nose like a ripe cherry. Blood spurted, and then ran in a steady stream down his upper lip into his mouth.

Martin shook his head, cursed, and wiped a sleeve across his nose. He lowered his head and charged Dolan like an enraged bull, his right fist sweeping out in a powerful blow that would have knocked Dolan down if it had landed. Willie Martin might have been the best fighter on F Ranch as Whooper Bill had said, but now, furious and in pain from his battered nose, he fought like a crazy man.

Dolan, moving swiftly, turned aside at exactly the right second and sledged Martin on the side of the head, sending him sprawling into the dust. Dazed, he lay there a moment, then got laboriously to his hands and knees. Again he wiped a sleeve across his bloody nose. He tipped his head back and glared at Dolan with the gut-deep hatred that one animal has for another.

"I'm going to kill you, bucko," Martin said.

He came on up to his feet and moved in, more slowly and cautiously this time. He kept one fist and forearm in front of his face for a time as he circled Dolan, then his rage and hatred overcame his caution and he rushed at Dolan, swinging both fists in wild blows that failed to land.

Dolan ducked and moved in close and shot a short, powerful punch to Martin's face. Martin grunted as he took the blow, but he didn't back up. Somehow he managed to catch Dolan's shoulder as he fell forward. He gripped it hard with his left hand, trying to hold Dolan with it while he hit him with his right.

Martin succeeded in throwing one punch that landed high on the side of Dolan's head. Dolan raised a knee and drove it hard into Martin's crotch. The storekeeper's grip on Dolan's shoulder slackened. Dolan jerked free and stepped back. Martin bent forward, whimpering in agony, completely helpless for that moment. Dolan hit him with a downsweeping fist on the back of the neck, a powerful blow that would have killed a lesser man. Martin dropped forward, his face in the dust, and didn't move.

Dolan swiped his face with a sleeve, staring down at the fallen man, then he shrugged. Stooping, he caught Martin by a shoulder and rolled him over. He said, "You're selling Kendall any supplies he wants. Savvy? Or do you need a little more persuading?"

Martin lay on his back, his eyes open, his arms thrown out on both sides of his chest. For a time he said nothing and he didn't move. Dolan brought a foot back to kick him in the ribs. Martin said, "Don't hit me again. I'm licked. He can have 'em. Any damned thing he wants."

"Get up," Dolan said.

Martin struggled to his feet and staggered to the porch and gripped a post with one hand. He felt of his nose very carefully with the other hand. Blood continued to drip from it. He said thickly, "I'm still gonna kill you, Buckskin. If I don't, Bronc Farrel will. You'll never live long enough to get out of the country."

He straightened, spat out a mouthful of blood, and started toward the corral. Dolan watched him reel like a drunk man until he reached the corral, then he strode to the wagons. Joel was sitting up. He grinned a little and winked when Dolan reached him.

"You made it look downright easy, Rafe," Joel said. "There was a time when I could have done the same thing, but, damn it, I just can't remember when the time comes that I'm too old to fight a man like Martin."

"Look," Bud exclaimed. "He's saddling up. He's leaving. You must have knocked all the fight out of him."

Dolan watched Martin mount and ride toward F Ranch, then he said, "Not quite all of it. He promised to kill me. Or if he didn't, Bronc Farrel would."

Joel gripped a wagon wheel and pulled himself to his feet. He felt his jaw and grimaced, then ran an exploratory hand over his belly. He said, "By God, he hits like a mule kicks. It feels like he hung my guts on my back ribs."

"You heard what I said, Joel?" Dolan demanded.

"I heard, all right, and you don't need to tell me what it means." Joel answered. "They'll know we're coming through the fence tomorrow and Farrel will have every man he's got right there at the gate to stop us."

"Maybe not," Dolan said thoughtfully. "They'll know we're coming, all right, so we won't surprise 'em, but I've got a hunch the men at the gate won't tell Farrel. The three fence riders Farrel's got are tough hands and they don't like me, so maybe they'll figure this is a good chance to take me and have all the fun themselves."

He looked at Sandy and her mother, thinking about the homestead family that had been turned back when he was riding fence, and what would have happened to the woman if he hadn't been there.

He said, "I don't think they'll get the best of us, but if they do, you women will be in trouble. If you've got any guns, you'd better have 'em ready."

"We aim to," Sandy said. "We're going to help fight our way through that fence."

Dolan glared at her, thoroughly outraged. "Oh no you won't. I never saw the day I'd let a woman do my fighting for me and I sure ain't starting in the morning. I'm talking about if we're dead. All four of us. If that happens, you'll need your guns to keep Farrel's men away from you and your mother."

Sandy began to swell up as she always did when she was thoroughly angry. She cried, "It's our fight, not yours. If you think you can keep Ma and me from doing our—"

"Harness your team, Lon," Dolan said curtly to him. "We'll load your wagon first. Maybe we won't need another one."

Lon nodded and motioned for Bud to go with him. Joel said, "Sandy, get a piece of paper and a pencil. We ain't stealing nothing. We'll keep a record of everything we take and we'll pay Farrel every nickel he's got coming."

Dolan had already started toward the store. Joel caught up with him, one hand pressed against his belly. He said, "She's a mite high-spirited, Rafe. By the time we've lived here a year or two, she won't be quite so spunky."

"I don't think she'll ever lose her spunk," Dolan said. "Looks to me like she's the kind who'll make out all right in this country."

He went into the store and lighted a lamp and set it on the counter. "Tell me what you want and I'll tote the stuff out to the porch, and Bud and his pa can load it."

Joel leaned against the counter and looked at the well-stocked shelves. "We'll start with flour. Sugar. Rice. Beans. Anything that looks good to you, Rafe. I reckon you'll be eating with us for a spell."

Dolan had started to lift a sack of flour, but now he set it back on the pile. "Joel, I aim to go as far as Antelope Spring. I don't aim to stay down there and plow your god-damned land for you. You're not making a farmer out of me."

"You're going to have to change your way of living," Joel said. "So'm I."

"Change all you want to," Dolan snapped, "but don't tell

me I've got to. You can't make a pussy cat out of a bob cat, and you're not going to civilize me."

"No, I guess nobody could civilize you," Joel conceded, "but time is gonna change you and there's not much you can do about it."

"Oh yes there is," Dolan said. "I can go to Canada or Alaska. Or Mexico if I have to. There's a whole big world I can go to."

Joel scratched the back of his neck. "I didn't allow that you'd do any plowing for us, but just getting us down there to Antelope Spring ain't enough. They'll try to run us off, which same you know. If you ain't there, I reckon they'll do it. Bud and Lon are farmers. They can take care of the plowing. We'll hire a crew of men if we can find 'em. You won't have to do a lick of work."

Dolan picked up the sack of flour, then set it back on the pile again. "It won't work, Joel. I'd just be sitting around on my hind end all day and eating my share of grub and not doing anything. Hell, I'd go crazy."

"You'd be hunting and scouting and fighting with Sandy," Joel said. "You'd find plenty to do."

"Won't work," Dolan said stubbornly.

He picked up the sack of flour for the third time and carried it to the porch and put it down. He heard the creak of the approaching wagon and heard Sandy call to Bud. Joel was right, he told himself.

Bronc Farrel would never accept their presence on what he considered his range unless he was thoroughly whipped or dead. He didn't think Farrel could be whipped. When he thought about Sandy and what would happen to her if Farrel's men ever had their way with her, he knew he had no choice.

The wagon reached the porch as Dolan turned back into the store. He pointed to a shelf of canned peaches. "You know, Joel, those peaches go mighty good when it's dry and I'm thirsty."

Joel nodded and grinned. "They do for a fact, Rafe. Let's take 'em."

CHAPTER 15

DOLAN WOKE before dawn and built a fire, then called the others. They straggled through the darkness, rubbing their eyes and yawning. The night had been a short one for sleeping. They had worked until midnight loading the wagon, with Sandy standing beside it keeping a record of every sack and barrel and can that went into the wagon.

The women started breakfast and the men took care of the horses. Joel moved slowly as if each motion hurt him. He would be days getting over the beating Martin had given him, Dolan thought, and wondered how effective he would be with a gun this morning.

As they finished eating, Dolan said, "Nobody has asked me why we're leaving so early, but I guess I'd better tell you. The three hardcases riding fence for Farrel are never in a hurry to get started. It might give us a little advantage if we got there while they're still sleeping or eating breakfast. Likewise we might get there before Farrel brings his men up, if they have sent for him."

No one spoke for a moment, but they were restless as if not wanting to think of what lay ahead for them. Joel poured another cup of coffee. Lon filled and lighted his pipe. Bud dropped his tin plate and cup into the wreck pan.

Joel had said Lon's wife was a great worrier, but so far Dolan hadn't heard her worry or complain about anything. She'd do her part, he thought. Somehow people had a way of meeting emergencies when it was time. Probably she'd worry her head off about trifles once they had met this crisis.

Sandy seemed the least restless of any of them. She said, her gaze fixed on Dolan, "What will we do if Farrel has all his crew at the gate?"

"There'll be too many to fight," Dolan said, "so we'll have to get tricky. Farrel's the kind of man who never thinks you're going to stand and fight. Not with long odds on his side, so we'll appear to cave in and drive away. We'll lay low as soon as we're out of sight, then along toward evening we'll swing in close to the end of the fence and cut the wires. If it comes to a fight, we'll just have his fence riders to buck."

"It would be better to do that in the first place than to bull it through like you're fixing to do," Sandy said sharply.

He shook his head. "No. Always take the direct way first. If that don't work, there's still plenty of time to get tricky."

She turned to Bud and said scornfully, "I suppose that's the man's way of doing things."

"Sure is." Bud winked at her. "The tricky way is the woman's way."

"One more thing," Dolan said. "Me and Joel will be riding in front. Bud, I want you and your dad in the lead wagon. Have your guns beside you so you can get at 'em quick. You women will drive the other two wagons. Stay behind by at least a quarter of a mile until I give the order to close up."

Sandy began to swell again as anger built in her. She said, "I refuse to stay behind a quarter of a mile."

"You will," Lon said in a tone that stopped the argument. "I guess there's some things Mr. Dolan will listen to us about, but there's some other things we'll listen to him and do what he says. This is one."

Dolan nodded, as surprised as anyone by Lon's firm tone. Human nature was never predictable, Dolan thought. Now that Lon and his wife knew they could not back out of this, they'd go ahead and do their share of the fighting if it was necessary. At least Dolan hoped that it would work that way, then told himself he was just wishing. In the long run it would be up to him and Joel. No sense fooling himself by thinking anything else.

"Let's get rolling," Dolan said curtly.

Sandy, perhaps shocked by the tone of her father's voice, was silent. As soon as the horses were harnessed and hooked up, Dolan and Joel mounted, Joel saying in a low voice, "You never know about a man, Rafe. I guess I figured Lon wrong."

"He'll do," Dolan said.

Still, he wasn't sure. He watched Bud climb to the seat of the lead wagon and pick up the lines; he saw Lon go around to the rear of the wagon and return to the front, wire clippers in his hands. He swung up beside Bud and said something. Bud nodded and spoke to the team. The horses leaned into their collars and the big wagon began to roll. Bud pulled in behind Joel, who was already riding south.

Dolan waited until he saw that Sandy and her mother were in their seats with the lines in their hands, then he touched up his horse and a moment later caught up with Joel. The sun was a red, half-circle above the eastern ridge, long shadows moving on the ground to the right of the horses and wagons.

The two men rode in silence, Dolan glancing obliquely at Joel and wondering what the old man was thinking. Perhaps he regretted bringing his son and his family out here. He shouldn't if he was thinking that. It was exactly as he had said a moment before. *You never knew about a man.*

Dolan had seen too many men who pretended to be brave end up as cowards. On the other hand, he had seen cases in which men who had been judged cowards had turned out to be heroes when the blue chip was down.

Glancing back, Dolan saw that Lon's wife had dropped behind as he had ordered, but Sandy had not obeyed. She was within fifty yards of the lead wagon. He swore softly and, wheeling his horse, galloped to her.

"In case you didn't savvy what I said—" Dolan began.

She leaned forward, her eyes sparkled by cold fury. "I savvied, all right, but I never told you I'd do what you said. I've got a gun, too. I'm a Kendall. If the Kendalls have to fight to get that great ranch you talk about, then we'll all fight. Being a woman or being a man has got nothing to do with it."

"Everybody but you agreed to let me run this party," Dolan said slowly, fighting to keep a tight rein on his temper, "and that's what I aim to do. You're going to agree to the same proposition, or I'll get off my horse and I'll pull you out of that seat. I'll turn you across my knees and I'll paddle your purty little butt till it's too sore to wiggle."

"If you as much as touch my purty little butt—" She stopped and tears began running down her cheeks. "Dolan, I never in all my life met a man who makes me as goddamned mad as you do."

"Are you going to stay a quarter of a mile behind the lead wagon like I said?" he demanded.

She couldn't say a word, but she nodded. Satisfied, he turned his horse and caught up with Joel.

"You know, I'm going to give that granddaughter of yours something to remember me by," Dolan said, "if she don't learn to follow orders."

Joel laughed softly. "Rafe, you don't know it yet, but she's the kind of woman you need. You've got to have somebody to bump heads with. You'd never be happy with a woman who jumped every time you yelled at her."

"I got the notion you figured I wouldn't do for Sandy's husband," Dolan said, irritated by the old man's words.

"That depends on whether you're willing to settle down and support her," Joel said. "Long as you're going to drift around like you have all your life and not be willing to work, why, hell, you wouldn't be a good husband for any woman."

"You're a fine one to talk about somebody else being a good husband," Dolan said.

Joel stared straight ahead, taking his time to respond. When he did, he only said, "I am for a fact," and let it go at that.

The sun was low in the east when they reached the fence, the air still holding the night chill. Dolan had seen a man standing on the other side of the gate, but they had been too far away to recognize him. Now he saw that the man was Willie Martin and that he had a rifle in his hands.

Dolan reined up and dismounted. He motioned for Bud to stop the wagon. He glanced at the tents, but he didn't see anyone else around the camp. This, he thought uneasily, didn't make any sense. He expected to see the three fence riders standing beside Martin if they were awake and out of bed. If they weren't, why was Willie Martin standing here as if he expected them?

Whooper Bill at least should be in sight. He always was when anyone approached the gate. Joel had swung down and moved up beside Dolan. Now both men walked slowly toward Martin, right hands brushing gun butts, wary eyes on Martin.

"Where's the fence riders?" Dolan asked.

Martin's gaze was fixed on Dolan. He ignored Lon and Bud in the wagon seat. He said, "I figgered you'd show up today and I'd have a chance to kill you just like I promised."

His nose was swollen and as purple as a ripe grape. Dolan

almost laughed when he looked at it and thought how much it must hurt. He said, "You got a purty good nose out of the fracas last night, didn't you, Willie?"

"One more good reason for me to kill you," Martin said. "I've rubbed out a few men in my time, but I never enjoyed it like I'm going to enjoy killing you. You'd better be glad the fence riders are already gone. They'd have fun putting a hole into your skull, too."

Martin's lips held a mocking smile. Dolan guessed the three fence riders hadn't left camp at all, but were in the big tent waiting for Martin's signal to cut loose. When that thought came to him, he reversed his decision to force a way through the fence. It was smarter to turn back rather than stand here and be cut down by three men he couldn't see.

"Well, I suppose you want to take your wagons through the gate," Martin said. "I'll unlock it. No sense of the rest of your outfit getting beefed, too. We'll settle for you."

"No," Dolan said. "We won't be going on through just now."

Martin had started toward the gate. Now he stopped, surprised. "What the hell! You've got one wagon here and the other two are coming. Why don't you want 'em to go through?"

Dolan never answered the question. Whooper Bill rushed out of the small tent, yelling, "Watch out, Rafe. Three of 'em are in the other tent. They're sticking their rifle barrels through holes in the canvas."

Martin cursed and started to turn, then stopped, keeping his eyes on Dolan.

"Call your friends out of the tent," Dolan said. "I figured this for an ambush."

"If it is," Bud said, "Martin gets the first slug."

"Show your faces," Martin called. "These gents want to look at 'em."

John L. Sullivan was the first to emerge from the big tent, then Concho, and finally Slim. "I'm surprised at you bastards," Dolan called to them. "I heard you brag for a month about what tough hands you were, but, hell, you're as yellow as they come, hiding in a tent so you could pick us off without being seen. Is that the way you've done all your killings?"

They shuffled toward the gate, their rifles on the ready. None of them said a word. Martin, still covered by Bud's Winchester, didn't know which way to move. Finally he said, "If you don't want that pup hurt, Dolan, call him off."

"No," Lon said sharply. "Nobody's calling anybody off. Martin, we're going through your fence because you're blocking a county road which same you don't have no right to do. We won't use your gate. Keep it locked."

"You try cutting that wire," Martin bellowed, "and you'll get a snootful of lead."

"So will you," Bud said.

This wasn't going the way Dolan had planned. It wasn't according to Martin's plan, either, but neither man could put the flow of action back on the track. Dolan realized things had gone too far now to avoid a showdown.

Dolan crouched, balanced easily, right hand splayed over the butt of his gun; he saw the bright whiteness of Martin's teeth as his lips parted. He heard someone snip a wire, then a faint whine as the taut wire shipped back. Dolan couldn't risk taking his eyes off Martin to see who had cut the wire, but he guessed it was Lon. The next instant John L. Sullivan pulled the trigger of his Winchester.

That shot triggered the fight. Dolan's gun was in his hand; he felt the familiar buck of the walnut butt against his palm, he saw the small blossom of gunflame flash into the early morning light, and through the rolling cloud of powder-smoke he saw John L. Sullivan take his first bullet and go down. Concho was next, catching Dolan's second bullet between the eyes.

Joel was firing beside Dolan. Now Martin was down, his legs going out from under him as quickly as if an invisible rope had jerked him off his feet. Dolan heard the sharp crack of the Winchester from the wagon seat and guessed it was Bud who had brought the big man down.

Slim was the last to fall. He was on his hands and knees, his gun that had fallen from his fingers was somewhere on the grass in front of him. He groped for it, found it, and lifted it as Dolan lined his gun on him and shot him through the head.

Martin rolled over to his stomach as Bud came down off his seat and ran to his father. Joel had holstered his revolver and he, too, was running toward Lon as Martin struggled to tip his .45 to an upward angle to shoot Dolan.

"Don't do it, Martin," Dolan ordered.

Slowly Martin lowered the gun barrel and then let go of the butt. Dolan called, "Bill, come and get this piece of carrion before I'm overcome by my temptation to shoot the son of a bitch."

Whooper Bill ran to Martin and helped him to his feet. Blood poured down his leg from a bullet hole in his thigh. For just a moment his face was so distorted that Dolan had the weird feeling a complete stranger was standing before him.

"You'll see the day you'd wished you'd killed me," Martin said, and then, leaning heavily on Whooper Bill, limped toward the small tent.

"Pull the bodies inside, Bill," Dolan called. "You and the cook stay here till I get word to Farrel."

He wheeled and ran to where Bud and Joel were kneeling beside Lon. He thought again of what Joel had said early that morning: "You never know about a man."

He wondered if Lon had foreseen what would happen when he'd got down from the wagon and cut that wire.

CHAPTER 16

LON LAY with both hands pressed against his belly. Blood seeped through his fingers and bubbled at the corners of his mouth. Joel rose and looked at Dolan and shook his head. He had seen too many men hit exactly as Lon was hit to even hope there was any chance for him, but Bud had never seen a man die from a bullet wound and he was saying, "Don't move, Dad. Ma and Sandy will be here in a minute. They'll know what to do."

Both women had pulled their teams to a stop and had stepped to the ground and were running to Lon. Sandy reached her father first and, kneeling beside him, cradled his head in her lap.

"You're not going to die, Pa," she said. "Not when we've got a ranch to build."

Ruth Kendall was beside him then. She knelt on the other side and kissed him. She whispered, "You're a brave man, Lon. I love you."

He raised a hand and gently touched her cheek. "I love you, too, Ruth. I love all of you." Sandy wiped the blood from his mouth. He whispered, "You can drive through the fence now."

The knowledge of death was in his eyes. Dolan, looking down at him, had the answer to the question he had asked himself a moment before. Lon Kendall had known exactly what would happen when he'd cut that wire. Perhaps it had been his way of committing suicide.

"It's getting dark," Lon breathed. "It won't be long now till I'll see the light."

A moment later he was gone. His lips parted and his eyes were filled with the vacant expression of death. Sandy eased his head to the ground and rose, then she began to cry. Bud walked to the fence and picked up the clippers. He cut the other two wires and, striding back to the wagon, tossed the clippers inside.

Ruth Kendall leaned forward and folded Lon's arms across his chest, then she rose. She said, "I've got something to say to all of you." She motioned toward Dolan. "You, too, Mr. Dolan."

"Ruth, maybe this ain't the time—" Joel began uneasily.

"This is exactly the time," she said, "and I'm going to say it now. We didn't want to come out here, Lon and me. We didn't have much back in Nebraska, but we had friends and we weren't afraid. You made us come."

She looked squarely at Joel, who began to fidget, dragging a boot toe back and forth through the dust, his gaze on the ground at his feet. "I didn't do no such thing, Ruth," he muttered. "I told you what I'd do for you. That's all. Lon was willing to come."

"Sure he was," she said, her eyes bright and hard. "Oh yes, he was willing to come because there never was a day in his life when Lon could stand up to you. You sent us money. I guess we'd have starved without it. I know we would have lost the Nebraska place if it hadn't been for your money. All the time Lon took it, he hated himself and called himself a failure. Maybe he was by your standards, but he was a good husband and a good father, and he should never have been made to feel he was a failure."

"My God, Ruth," Joel cried in agony. "I never said anything like that to Lon in my life."

"You never said it, but you thought it, and he knew you thought it." She turned her gaze to Sandy, who was standing on the other side of the body, then at Bud, who remained beside the wagon. "Even his own children considered him a failure. They never said so, neither, but he knew how they felt, and he knew how it made him look when they compared him to their grandfather."

She swallowed and almost broke down, but she took a long breath and hurried on, "We came because we couldn't argue with you." She had turned her gaze back to Joel. "You have money. You helped Lon sell our farm. You decided what was best for us. You were the one who made the decision every day about how far we would travel. You picked every camp ground. Well, maybe that was the way it had to be, but I knew how it hurt Lon. All we had to do was to say yes and sit on our wagon seat and drive our team."

She bowed her head and lowered her gaze to Lon's body, a great sob shaking her, but no tears came. She regained her self-control a moment later and went on, "I broke down yesterday after we crossed the summit. I didn't know about this fence then and that we had to fight our way through it, but I was scared just like I've always been scared of things that are new to me. I couldn't face it. I told Lon I was going to kill myself. He hugged me and patted me on the back and said no, that wasn't the way. It didn't solve anything and it didn't help anybody.

"He didn't want to live any more than I did. I didn't know how it had been working on him all the way out here till he told me, but he said he couldn't face it, either. Then he told me that he'd lived as long as he wanted to, but he had learned one thing on the trip. He said he was going to do something for his children, that when he died he'd do it the right way and some good would come out of it.

"I don't know what he did just now, but he was murdered and the fence is down and we're going on to Antelope Spring. I'm not afraid anymore. Not the way I have been all my life because I don't care whether I live or not, now that Lon's gone. There's nothing to be afraid of anymore. If you squeeze a sponge dry, there just ain't any sense in going on squeezing it."

She pointed a finger at Bud. "You get the canvas out of your wagon and wrap your father in it. Let's get through that fence before somebody stops us. We're going to bury him beside Antelope Spring."

Ruth and Sandy walked to the wagons and climbed to the seats. Bud and Sandy were crying, but Bud got the canvas as his mother had told him to do. He wrapped Lon's body in it and carried him to the wagon, then he, too, climbed into the seat and picked up the lines.

Joel mounted, swiping a hand across his face. Dolan said, "Give me the list of supplies we took from the store. I'm going to stop at Farrel's ranch and I'll give it to him. You stay on the road. I'll catch you before you reach the spring."

Joel nodded and handed the folded piece of paper to him.

Joel rode through the gap in the fence, the wagons stretching out behind him. Dolan stood beside his horse, one hand on the saddle horn, and stared at the wagons, then he mounted. He would have caught up with the wagons and passed them if Whooper Bill had not emerged from the small tent and called, "Rafe."

Dolan reined his horse toward the old buckaroo. He stopped and looked down at him. He said, "Thanks for warning me. It was purty risky."

"I figured you'd smelled a rat and knowed where them boogers was hiding, but I couldn't stay inside the damned, stinking tent any longer. I had to be sure you knowed."

"Thanks," Dolan said again, and wondered why the old man had called to him.

Whooper Bill ran the tip of his tongue over dry lips. The air was still cold, but he was sweating. He jerked his bandanna out of his pants pockets and wiped his face, then he blurted, "Can you use a worn-out old buckaroo when you get to Antelope Spring?"

Surprised, Dolan said, "Well, I dunno—"

"Let me tell you how it was," Whooper Bill cut in. "When Martin rode in last night, he had a disposition like a sore-tailed grizzly. He took the gate key away from me, and then he worked it out with the fence riders what they'd do this morning when you showed up. They was gonna wait till you and the wagons got through the gate and got close enough to the big tent so the bastards inside couldn't miss you, then they was gonna gun down all you men and screw the women. This morning Martin made me stay inside the tent. He said he'd kill me if I showed my face outside."

"It was riskier than I figured," Dolan said, "you warning me like you did."

"Risky enough if the shooting had gone the other way," Whooper Bill said. "Only I figgered you'd take 'em, which you done. That old goat standing beside you didn't do much good, but the kid in the wagon put Martin down."

Whooper Bill swallowed, then went on, "I didn't think I'd ever live to say this, but I ain't gonna work for Bronc no more. He's gone loco. Maybe it's on account of his bitchy wife. Or maybe because he knows he can't hang on much longer, holding by guns what he can't hold legal like. Anyhow, this fence was a bad idea. Hiring men like them fence riders was worse. Sending Martin to the store to beat old man Hodig up was just plain mean. Hell, I'm gonna quit him, but I'd like to work for you. I guess I don't want to leave the country."

"I thought you were too bunged up to ride," Dolan said.

"I can still do part of a day's work," Whooper Bill said. "It kind o' depends on the weather, too. When it's dry and warm, I do purty good. Anyhow, you need somebody who knows the country and where you can buy cattle and how to build them stockade corrals and—"

"All right, Bill," Dolan interrupted. "You come on down to Antelope Spring later on today. You'd better stop and tell Farrel about Martin and then come on."

"That's what I aimed to do," Whooper Bill said, bobbing his head. "Likewise I can still shoot a gun and you're sure gonna need all the guns you can get or Bronc'll just run over you."

"I don't pay the crew," Dolan said, "but I'll see we find a place for you."

Dolan rode south, wondering if he should have taken Whooper Bill with him. It was hard to tell what Farrel would do if he knew Bill was quitting him. But maybe he'd fire Bill and not ask what he was going to do.

When Dolan caught up with the wagons and rode past them, he intended to go on to F Ranch, but Joel motioned for him to pull in beside him. He asked, "Any reason you can't ride with me as far as Farrel's ranch and catch up with us after that?"

"No."

"I'd like it if you would do that," Joel said.

Dolan looked sharply at the old man, thinking that it was the first sign of weakness he had seen. He waited, riding beside Joel in front of Bud's wagon. Presently Joel turned his head, and Dolan, glancing at him again, saw agony in his eyes, the agony of a man who was being torn apart by the memory of something he had done and could not undo.

"He knew what I thought of him," Joel said in a low tone, "but I never told him. I never criticized anything he ever done, neither. How did he know, Rafe?"

Now that Lon Kendall was dead, Dolan knew there was

nothing in the world he could say that would take the pain of guilt away from Joel Kendall.

"I don't know, Joel," Dolan said. "I just don't know."

CHAPTER 17

Dolan rode beside Joel until they reached the turnoff to F Ranch. He said, "I'll catch up with you before long," and reined to his right. He saw that Farrel had just pulled gear from his chestnut and had turned the animal into the corral. He started toward the house, but when he saw Dolan, he stopped and waited for him.

Dolan pulled up when he reached Farrel. He said, "I met a friend of mine at your store. I told you about him, Joel Kendall. He's got three wagons and his family and he's settling at Antelope Spring."

Farrel took the news without showing the slightest change of expression. "You're with him, I suppose?" he said.

"I'll stay with him awhile," Dolan said, "just in case you get proddy and Joel needs another gun. That's why I rode in here to tell you. I want to know your intentions."

"You know them without me telling you," Farrel said. "You know damned well I'll get proddy. I'll get so proddy I won't stand for it. Where are they now?"

Dolan motioned to the south. "They're on their way. They'll be at the Springs in a couple of hours or so."

"How did you get through the fence?"

Dolan told him what had happened, adding, "Martin's hit pretty bad. You'd better send a wagon for him."

Still Farrel's expression did not change. He asked, "Have you got any women in your party?"

"Two."

"Get them to safety. I don't want to be responsible for the death of any women, so I'm warning you. Or turn your whole outfit back so they'll be off my range by night."

"Joel Kendall can't turn back any more than you can," Dolan said, "which means you'll find us at Antelope Spring."

"You won't be there long," Farrel said.

He wheeled and strode toward his stone office. Dolan rode up to him and handed him the sheet of paper that Sandy had used to record the supplies Joel had bought. "Joel took these items from the store. Figure their value and send the bill to him. He wants to pay for them."

"He'll get the bill and he'll pay," Farrel said, "but not in gold."

He took the paper without slackening his steps and disappeared into the stone building. Dolan whirled his horse and started back to the road, but Liz ran out of the house and stopped him. She stood in front of his horse, her head tipped back. Dolan reined up, swearing softly. The last thing he wanted now was trouble with Farrel over his wife.

"Don't be in such a hurry, Dolan," she said. "I didn't think I'd see you again."

"I had business with your husband," Dolan said curtly. "Get out of the way."

"It must have been important business to bring you here," she said. "I thought Bronc ordered you out of the country."

"I wanted to show him I wasn't going to obey his orders." Dolan hesitated, wondering if she would ever hear about the gunfight at the gate. He decided Farrel might not tell her and it would be a good thing if she knew about it. He told her, adding, "He'll probably hit us tonight or tomorrow. I guess you know what that will mean."

"I know, all right." She moved forward and laid a hand on his leg. "Take me with you, Dolan. I can't stay here. He'll kill me. I hate him. My God, I didn't think I could ever hate a man the way I hate him. I want to see him dead."

Dolan shook his head. "I can't take you with me and you know it. That would give him an excuse to come at us shooting, and I don't aim to give him any excuse." He nodded at her. "So long."

He rode on, wondering if she really was in danger or if this was her way of turning other men against her husband. One thing she had said he did believe, that she wanted Bronc Farrel dead.

"Dolan!" she screamed, running after him. "Dolan! I want to tell you something."

He stopped and looked back at her, not sure whether he was smart or a fool to talk to her anymore. In the end she might turn out to be an ally, and the way things were shaping up, Joel would need all the allies he could get. For three men and two women to make a stand against the F Ranch crew was nothing short of suicide.

She was out of breath when she reached him. As soon as she could talk, she said, "You know you haven't got a chance against Bronc. They'll kill every one of you, including the women if they're helping you fight."

"He won't have much crew left if he does that," Dolan said.

"Don't be an idiot," she said. "It wouldn't stop him for a minute. You know that. He can always hire more men. What I wanted to tell you was that if Bronc gets killed, the outfit comes to me. If I owned F Ranch, you and your friends wouldn't have any trouble settling at Antelope Spring." She paused, and added significantly, "He's alone now."

This was exactly like her, he thought. He turned his horse and rode away without a word. Maybe he'd run into bitchier women than Liz Kendall, but he couldn't remember when it had been.

He caught up with the wagons, nodded at Ruth Kendall as he rode past her, then Sandy, and finally at Bud. When he reined in beside Joel, the old man shot him a quick glance, asking, "Learn anything?"

"Not much I didn't know already," Dolan answered. "We can expect them to hit us before long. In the morning, probably. He said for us to get our women to safety. He didn't want to be responsible for their deaths."

"Where could we take them where they'd be safe?"

Dolan shook his head. "I dunno. Back north of the fence, I guess."

"How many men will he bring?"

"Depends on what he thinks he needs to do the job. If he fetches his whole crew, he'll have about twenty men."

Joel groaned. "We'll have to make a deal with him, Rafe. We can't fight that big an outfit."

"The only deal he'd make with you is for you to keep right on rolling toward the Nevada line," Dolan said, "and you won't do that."

"No," Joel agreed grimly. "I won't do that."

When they reached the cottonwoods below Antelope Spring, Ruth was the first to step to the ground. She looked at the swift-flowing, clear stream, then she turned completely around and for a moment stared at the desert to the west.

Dolan sat his saddle, watching her, a little uneasy as she turned and walked away. After what she had said at the fence, he guessed she was capable of saying anything. The others must have had the same thought because they did not step down until she had found the place she was looking for.

"We'll bury Lon here," she said, indicating a spot on the bench east of the stream where the water would never reach it. "Right now we'll put a cross up, but later on we'll build a fence around the grave so the cattle can't tromp on it. We'll get a gravestone later on, too, with his name and the date and everything."

Joel dismounted, calling, "Bud, get the shovels out of Sandy's wagon. We'll start digging right away."

"I'll take care of the horses," Dolan said.

Ruth said something to Sandy. The girl took an ax from her wagon and the two women walked into the cottonwoods. By the time Dolan finished stripping harness from the teams and gear from the saddle horses, and had watered and staked them out, Joel and Bud had the grave nearly finished. Joel was leaning on his shovel handle, so tired he had trouble lifting a shovelful of dirt to the top of the grave. Dolan slid down beside him and took the shovel. He worked beside Bud until Joel, standing at ground level above them, said it was deep enough.

Ruth came to the grave, a Bible in her hand. She said, "Bring the body."

Dolan walked beside Bud to the wagon that held the body, thinking the mouse had become a lioness. Perhaps it was the first time in her life that she was in position to give orders and be sure that Joel would obey them.

She had a mean streak in her, Dolan thought, or she wouldn't have said what she had at the fence. She had hurt Joel, which was exactly what she had meant to do; she had admitted she and Lon had needed the money he had sent, and then had driven the knife into him as deeply as she could. What she had done to Sandy and Bud was even worse. They still had most of their lives ahead of them, and they would remember what she had said as long as they lived.

He took Lon's feet and Bud the head. They carried the body, still wrapped in the canvas, to the grave and lowered it to the ground. Dolan stood beside Bud on one side of the grave, Joel and Sandy on the other, their heads bare while Ruth read from the Bible, ending with the Twenty-third Psalm. She recited the Lord's Prayer, then stood in silence for a long time, staring at the blue sky before she finally said, "Lord, we give our beloved husband and son and father into Thy keeping." She walked away quickly, her head bowed.

Dolan and Bud picked up the body and eased it into the grave, then filled it, smoothing the mound of earth so no one could misunderstand or question what it was. When they were done, Sandy brought the cross she and her mother had made and drove it into the soft dirt at the head of the grave. Joel had built a fire beside the creek and Ruth had started supper.

For a moment Sandy and Bud looked at each other, then Sandy turned to Dolan. "What makes a man like Pa do what he did and get killed. He knew it would happen, didn't he?"

Dolan nodded. "He knew, all right. I wondered at first about it, but I'm sure now he knew. I don't know how he knew, or why he did it. Maybe it was like your Ma said. He didn't want to live any longer. I guess everybody wants his life to mean something, and this was his way of making his mean something."

"I didn't think we were bad to him," Bud said.

He sounded as if he were a small boy. Dolan, glancing at him, saw that he was close to crying. Sandy was, too, but she managed to say, "He was a failure as far as making a living for us was concerned. Ma knows it, too. She wasn't one bit better."

"That's probably why she said it," Dolan told her. "Don't take what she said too hard."

Impulsively Sandy reached out and laid a hand on his arm. "Thank you," she said. "I needed someone to say that to me."

For a moment their eyes met and for the first time since

he had met her, he sensed she felt no hostility toward him, then she turned away and walked to the fire. "It's gonna be hard to forget what Ma said," Bud muttered bitterly. "Hard as hell on Grandpa, too. He don't deserve it, damn it. He's done the best he could for us."

Dolan and Bud walked to where Joel was standing at the edge of the creek looking down at the clear, swirling water. He said, "It's good drinking water, Rafe. About as good as I ever tasted. I remember just how this place looked when I rode through here. It was a long time ago, but I remember."

"It is good water," Dolan agreed.

"You want the tents put up, Grandpa?" Bud asked.

Joel nodded. "Yeah, we'd best put 'em up as soon as we finish supper." He said to Dolan, "We didn't use 'em much on the way out here. We had clear weather most of the time, but we're gonna have to live in 'em now." He rubbed his face, and added, "God, there's so much to do. What about lumber, Rafe? Can we get it, or have we got to build log cabins out o' them cottonwoods?"

Dolan saw that he wasn't considering the possibility that he might not live long enough to put up any buildings. Dolan said, "There's a sawmill in the Blue Mountains, but it's a long ways from here."

"We'll haul the lumber if we can get it," Joel said. "It'll last longer'n cottonwood logs and make us a tighter house."

"Come and get it," Sandy called.

They turned toward the fire. Dolan wondered how soon Ruth Kendall would crack up. He didn't believe she could go on this way much longer and it would be up to Sandy to do what had to be done. It had been his opinion for years that white women were a bitchy lot. He had never found one he enjoyed sleeping with; he had never even found one he liked. Liz Farrel confirmed that opinion, and Ruth hadn't done anything to contradict it, but he had a feeling Sandy was different.

CHAPTER 18

A SENSE of impending disaster hovered over them all through supper. The women ate very little. Dolan wasn't sure whether it was grief over Lon's death or worry about their future that had taken their appetite. Dolan's concern was for their safety, and he didn't know what could be done for them. He could insist that they be moved away from camp, but it might be more dangerous for them to be alone than to be here.

As soon as Joel finished eating, he walked away from the fire. Dolan caught up with him, saying, "I've been worrying about the women. I thought we could move 'em across the creek so they wouldn't be here when the shooting starts, but then they might be worse off than ever. There's a bunch of Paiutes back on Steens Mountain somewhere. I wouldn't trust any of Farrel's men who might run on to 'em, either."

Joel nodded. "Leave 'em here. I don't think they'd go if we told 'em to." He filled his pipe, his eyes on the distant rim of the desert to the west. "Rafe, a man can think he's doing what's best for everybody and be dead wrong. The one thing I never figgered on was Lon getting killed."

"You had no reason to figure on it," Dolan said a little impatiently. "No sense torturing yourself about something you couldn't help."

"I know it," Joel said glumly, "but I keep on doing it no matter what I tell myself."

"I never knew you to do it before."

"I never had a family to think of before," Joel said, "or a woman who'd dig her claws into me. I didn't expect it of Ruth."

"Let's help Bud put the tents up," Dolan said. "It'll give you something to do. Then we'd better think about how we're going to beat Farrel's bunch off when they come."

Joel nodded and without a word turned to the wagon that held the tents. It was dusk by the time they finished. A storm was moving in from the west, the dark clouds dimming the already fading light. Lightning threw its jagged spears at the earth, and thunder rolled toward them like the sound of distant cannons. It was raining hard out there somewhere on the desert, for the wind carried the scented smell of sage to them.

"Somebody's riding in," Bud said. "I'll get my Winchester."

Dolan had seen the rider top the ridge to the north and had been watching him. He said, "Don't do that. It's Whooper Bill Munk. He's a friend of mine. He's been working for Farrel, but he wants to throw in with us."

"How do you know we can trust him?" Joel demanded suspiciously.

"How do you know you can trust me?" Dolan asked. "I worked for Farrel, too."

"Oh hell, that's different," Joel snapped. "I knew you before we got here."

"You'll have to take my word for it," Dolan said. "You're paying the bills, but I've got the right to make some decisions, and I have decided we need Whooper Bill."

Joel grunted something, then said grudgingly, "All right, if you say so."

"I say so," Dolan said. "Bud, fetch in enough wood to get breakfast. Throw it into one of the tents so if we get a gully washer, we'll have some that's dry. The rain may not amount to anything, but you can't tell."

Bud picked up the ax and walked away. Ruth had gone into one of the tents, leaving Sandy to finish up. Whooper Bill rode in a few minutes later. Dolan introduced him to Joel. The two old men shook hands, both instinctively disliking the other. They were like two roosters, Dolan thought, both past their prime and not wanting to admit it or even let anyone else see it. Whooper Bill would do all the riding that anyone asked of him if it killed him, Dolan thought.

"Have I got a job?" Whooper Bill asked, looking Joel in the eyes.

"Rafe says so," Joel said.

Whooper Bill thought about it a moment, still staring at Joel as if not sure he was saying yes or no, then shrugged as if deciding it was yes and there was no sense in pushing for a more positive answer.

"I was late getting here," Whooper Bill said, turning back to Dolan. "I stayed with Martin till a wagon showed up to take him to F Ranch. Then I stopped to tell Bronc I was quitting him and he got madder'n I ever seen him before. It wasn't that he wanted me to keep working for him. No sirree, he was glad to get rid of me. It was when I told him I was coming here and throwing in with you that he went plumb out of his head. He hit me, Rafe. By God, he hit me right across the mouth. He promised to hang me if I signed on with you."

"And me beside you, on the same limb," Dolan said.

"Yep, that's what he promised." Whooper Bill took a long breath. "I tell you, Rafe, he just ain't the same man I came up the trail from California with."

"What changed him?" Joel asked, suddenly interested in what Whooper Bill was saying.

"I dunno what changes a man," Whooper Bill said thoughtfully. "Maybe he's been listening to the wrong feller. Maybe he took on a wife who's a bitch and she's turned him inside out. Both true." He sucked in another long breath and went on, "And mebbe he's just got too big for his britches and got boogery, knowing he ain't gonna be able to hold on to all the range he's claiming. I guess it's a little of all three."

"I'd say it was," Dolan said. "I'm not real proud of myself, but he fooled me completely when I first met him. It wasn't long till I saw he was like all the other cowmen I've run into, so greedy he never had a thought about anybody but himself."

"Whatever it was," Whooper Bill said, "he's sent for every man he's got and they'll be riding in here tomorrow morning. Was I you, I'd move them wagons into a half circle so you'll have some protection. It'd be a little help. Not much, but a little."

Joel bristled instinctively, plainly not wanting any suggestions from Whooper Bill. Dolan said quickly, "That's a good idea. I'll harness a team and pull the wagons around like you said."

"I'll give you a hand," Joel said, still not liking it.

"Had your supper, Bill?" Dolan asked.

"No, but I ain't hungry after having that set-to with Bronc," said Whooper Bill. "I'll have a cup of coffee, though, if you've got any left."

"How about it, Sandy?" Dolan called. "Any coffee left?"

"Sure is," the girl answered. "Half a pot."

"Sandy, meet the new member of our crew, Whooper Bill Munk," Dolan said. "Bill, this purty little thing is Sandy Kendall, Joel's granddaughter."

"Pleased to meet you, Whooper," Sandy said, "but I'm not just a purty little thing."

"I know," Dolan said. "You're a complete, growed-up woman."

"Well now," Whooper Bill said, "she's purty and that's a fact."

Sandy looked at him sharply. "If you meant that, I'll accept it as a compliment, but if you're pulling my leg, I'll put poison in your coffee."

Whooper Bill sighed and winked at Dolan. "She's a fireball." He turned to Sandy. "Ma'am, an old man like me would never pull a purty girl's leg."

"Oh, I'm not so sure about that," She had poured his coffee and handed the cup to him. "Here you are. Wet your whistle."

"Thank you kindly," Whooper Bill said, and hunkered beside the fire as he drank his coffee."

Dolan strode rapidly to where Joel was harnessing one of the teams. When he reached him, the old man said, "He's a know-it-all, that old goat."

"He's got some good ideas whether you like him or not," Dolan said, thinking that Joel was being childishly petty about it. "Later on if you don't like him, you don't have to keep him, but he's another rifle and that's one thing we need right now."

Joel grunted and dropped the matter. After the wagons were drawn into a semicircle on one side of the tents with the stream on the other, Joel led the horses back to where they had been staked out and stripped off their harness. Bud came in with several armloads of wood and threw them down inside the tent the men would occupy.

Dolan introduced Bud to Whooper Bill, who was on his second cup of coffee. As soon as Joel returned to the fire, Dolan said, "We'd better put out guards tonight. Bud, you take it till midnight. Bill, you take the next turn. Wake me up at three. I'll take it until sunup."

"You're leaving me out," Joel said angrily. "Damn it, I can take my turn as well—"

"Sure you can," Dolan said. "The point is you'd better get some sleep. Tomorrow you've got to see well enough to shoot straight."

Joel shrugged and let it go. It had been the worst kind of a day for him, Dolan knew. He was not surprised that Joel remained by the fire after Bud had picked up his rifle and disappeared into the darkness, and Whooper Bill had rolled up in his blanket in one of the tents. The storm had moved by to the south with only a faint sprinkle. Lightning still flickered along the horizon, thunder so muted by distance that it was only a faint rumble.

Dolan hunkered beside Joel, sensing that the old man needed his companionship for a few minutes before he went to sleep. Lon's death and Ruth's words had shaken him so that his self-confidence had been momentarily destroyed. He filled his pipe and fired it with a burning twig, then glanced obliquely at Dolan.

"Do you believe in anything, Rafe?" Joel asked.

Dolan didn't answer for a time. It was the question he had not expected Joel to ask and it shocked him. Joel Kendall had never been a man to examine his abilities or to inquire into anyone's belief. The question simply didn't fit him.

"Yeah, I believe in a lot of things," Dolan answered finally, not sure that he was saying what needed to be said. "I believe in myself. I believe I've got certain rights in this country, and by God, I'm going to fight for 'em if I have to." He laughed shortly. "Joel, I've never been one to work as you've been happy to point out to me, or a man to feel responsibility to anyone else, but I'm seeing things different than I used to. I aim to cut Bronc Farrel down to size, partly because he tried to tell me what I could or couldn't do, and I don't allow any man to do that, and partly because he's got no right to keep you or anybody else off land that don't belong to him."

Joel nodded grimly. "You're changing, Rafe. I knew you would, once you got into this game."

"I dunno how much I'm changing," Dolan said, "but I've

passed up some good fights with cowmen. I hate the whole damned lot of 'em. I decided I wasn't going to pass this fight up, and I wasn't going to be kicked around anymore."

Joel nodded again, then asked, "You believe in anything else?"

"I believe in God, if that's what you're trying to get me to say," Dolan answered, "but not the kind of God I used to hear the preachers scream about when I was a kid. He's a good God. I've heen Him in nature and I doubt that the preachers have. Sure, nature can be wicked, but it's mostly in the way you treat it and the way you let it treat you." Dolan got to his feet and slapped Joel on the back. "I've got to get some sleep. We'll whip Farrel tomorrow. I'm not sure how, but we will. That's something else I believe."

After he lay down with his head on his saddle, he saw Joel's gaunt figure still beside the fire. Just before he dropped off to sleep, he realized why Joel had asked what he had. He was thinking of Bud. Sandy, too. They both might be killed, and that would be a loss he could never accept if he survived. It would kill him and be another debt to collect from Bronc Farrel.

CHAPTER 19

FARREL DID NOT attack during the night. Dolan had not thought he would. When he returned to camp after standing guard, the dawn light was strong enough to see the ridge to the north. Joel had started a fire. He seemed more hollow-eyed and gaunt than ever.

Looking at him, Dolan thought how much he had changed in the few hours since they had met in Willie Martin's store. Joel had been old and tired and covered with trail dust, but he had been in command, still as sure of himself as he had always been. He wasn't in command now. He looked at Dolan and tried to force a smile, but it refused to come to his lips.

"Morning, Rafe," Joel said. 'See anything or hear anything?"

"Nothing," Dolan answered, "but they'll come. I'm not just sure how, though. If they come riding in hard, shooting as they come, we'll get under the wagons and cut down as many as we can. There's six of us. We can do a hell of a lot of damage before they get to us, maybe enough to discourage 'em."

He didn't really believe that, but he wanted Joel to think he did. Joel nodded. "Maybe," he said.

"But if they come in slowlike and want to palaver," Dolan went on, "I'll move to the other side of the wagons and I'll palaver with 'em. You'll be on the ground under the wagons ready to cut loose if Farrel starts the ball, but I'll let Farrel know he'll be the first to get it when the fireworks start."

Joel nodded again. He said, "All right." He turned to the tent that held the women. "Ruth! Sandy! Time to start cooking."

No, he wasn't in command now, Dolan thought. Forty-eight hours ago he would have insisted on standing in front of the wagons beside Dolan. Now he was quite willing to follow Dolan's lead.

A few minutes later the women came out of their tent, Ruth tired and red-eyed, Sandy buoyant and happy, her face washed, her hair brushed and tied at the back of her neck. If the girl had the slightest worry about the future, she gave no indication of it.

Whooper Bill and Bud joined them a few minutes later. Whooper Bill glowering at Joel one second and smiling at Sandy the next, Bud rubbing his eyes and complaining about getting up in the middle of the night instead of waiting for morning.

By the time they finished breakfast, the sun had tipped up over Steens Mountain, slowly wiping out the shadow that had entirely covered the desert a few minutes before.

"We're staying here until we see what happens," Dolan said. "They'll show up before long. Bronc Farrel's not a man to wait when he's got a job like this to do. Just be sure you have your Winchesters within reach, Joel, you'd better lay out all the shells you've got. We don't want to be running around under fire trying to find our ammunition."

"I'll get it," Joel said. "Bud, gimme a hand."

"One thing," Dolan said. "The bank of the creek is high enough to give you women protection. When Farrel and his outfit show up, you can—"

"No," Sandy said angrily. "When they show up, we're shooting the same as anybody else. I thought you understood that."

"I did, which same didn't mean I liked the idea," Dolan said, "but maybe you'd be better off getting shot than being taken alive if we lose the fight. We can use two extra rifles, all right. You and Mrs. Kendall stay under that end wagon." He pointed to the wagon on his right. "Bud, you stay under the one on the left. Joel and Whooper Bill, the middle wagon. When the fireworks start, hug the ground except when you're shooting. Don't get up and start walking around under any circumstances."

"And just where will you be?" Sandy asked with feigned concern.

She was still angry, Dolan thought. He grinned at her. "Sandy, you're a purty little thing when you're mad."

She began to swell up the way she always did when a

sudden burst of anger struck her, but before she could say a word, Bud shouted, "Here they come."

Dolan wheeled, his gaze sweeping the ridge line to the north. Two men had just dropped over the crest and were trotting down the slope toward the wagons. Two other men showed behind them, and then a third pair.

"Get under the wagons," Dolan ordered. "That's Bronc Farrel in the lead. His ramrod, Pete Larkin, is riding beside him. Looks like they're aiming to palaver, so I'll oblige 'em. Just be sure none of you start the ball. That's my privilege."

Picking up his Winchester from where he had leaned it against a front wheel of the middle wagon, Dolan stepped between it and the next one to the right. He moved out twenty yards and stopped, his .30-.30 held on the ready.

As he waited, he thought about that morning over a month ago when he had watched Bronc Farrel, who had been riding the same chestnut gelding he was forking now, top the ridge and ride down the slope toward him, and how friendly Farrel had been, pretending to hold Larkin back and wanting to hire Dolan.

He'd been honest enough about that, Dolan told himself. The way Farrel looked at it, the cheapest and most effective way of dealing with a tough stranger who might become an enemy was to hire him. Well, Farrel had fooled him, all right, but it hadn't taken him long to see through the cowman. Now, thinking of Liz Farrel, Dolan wondered which one was to blame for their trouble. Probably both, for he judged that neither was willing to give an inch to the other.

Standing here waiting for the showdown while F Ranch hands kept pouring over the crest of the ridge, Dolan's pulse began to pound. He had faced death more times than he could remember, but never with the odds against him as great as they were now. The only chance he had for life depended on Farrel not wanting to die.

When two stubborn men were hell-bent on a collision course, one or both will probably end up dead. Dolan had no illusions about his own stubbornness, and from his experience with Bronc Farrel, he was convinced that the cowman was no more tractable than he was.

Farrel and Larkin reined up fifty feet in front of Dolan. Farrel dismounted, dignified, completely at ease. His men

were all on this side of the ridge now and were dividing into
two lines, one flanking Farrel on his left, the other moving
in on his right. Nobody else had stepped down.

Now Dolan understood Farrel's strategy, and he felt as
naked as the day he was born, standing out here in the open.
Farrel was in position to decide when the fireworks would
start. When they did, he could swing his gelding around to
protect him while his men charged forward, shooting as they
came. Dolan would be cut down in the first burst of gun-
fire, and it would take only a few more seconds to reach the
wagons and wipe out the five defenders.

"The last stand of the homesteaders," Farrel said with
cold sarcasm. "You're no fool, Dolan. You knew we'd
come, and you know that if you resist, we'll kill every one
of you. If that old fool of a Bill Munk is with you, we'll
hang him. I'll give you one minute to start your people
harnessing up. Take your wagons south. Don't come back
through my range."

Dolan had that cold-stone feeling in the bottom of his
belly that he'd felt a few times in his life when it looked as
if his luck had run out. He would never make his bluff stick,
but he had to try. He couldn't run now. He wouldn't get
halfway to the wagons before he'd be a dead man.

"Don't count that minute out by seconds just yet, Farrel," Dolan said. "Consider the proposition that I'll kill you
before you can smoke me down."

Farrel laughed shortly. "I don't think so, Dolan," he said,
and backed up a step, bringing his gelding around so that
the animal hid most of his body from Dolan.

"Hold your horses, Bronc," Whooper Bill called. "Before
you start throwing lead, take a look at the side of the hill.
The whole damn bunch of you will be smoked down the
minute you crack your first cap."

Farrel didn't move. His lips curled in derision as he started to say something, but Larkin shouted, "He's right, Bronc.
See for yourself."

Farrel turned his head to look and was plainly jolted by
what he saw. Then Dolan looked, and he saw the most
amazing sight of his life. The slopes of Steens Mountain
had suddenly sprouted Indians. Some were crouched in the
sagebrush, and some were partly hidden by boulders, but

they were visible, their rifles lined on the F Ranch men. There were thirty or more of them, Dolan guessed, enough to cut the buckaroos down in the first volley.

For the next twenty seconds or more, Farrel and Larkin and their riders remained frozen, eyes on the Paiutes as if this was something which could not be happening, but still could not be disregarded as if it were a nightmare.

Now a tall Indian moved to the edge of the cliff above the spring. He said something in the Paiute tongue which Dolan did not understand, but Whooper Bill did. He called, "I savvy their lingo, Bronc. I guess you remember that. Well, that there feller who just got done talking is Lokan. He's the chief of this here little party, and he's Scooter's pa. He says he wants to kill Larkin on account of what Larkin did to the boy, but he allows that if you git pronto, he'll let you all go. If you don't, he promises you you'll be dead men in about the time it takes to pull some triggers."

He was adding words to the chief's threat, Dolan thought. It was plain Farrel didn't believe it. He called to one of his men, "Shorty, what did he say?"

"Just about what Whooper Bill said except he didn't talk so much." The buckaroo turned his horse. "Time we was moving, Boss."

Farrel stepped into the saddle and jerked his head at Dolan. "I'm a patient man, so I can wait. There'll be another day if you stay here. The Paiutes just delayed your departure, but they didn't change anything."

Farrel whirled his horse and rode up the ridge, Larkin reining in beside him. Dolan waited to see that the buckaroos followed Farrel. When the last rider had disappeared over the crest of the ridge, he called, "Bill, come here. I want to talk to the chief."

Whooper Bill crawled out from under the wagon and started toward the Paiute chief, calling, "I figgered for a little while they was gonna ride right over us." Dolan ran after him and caught up with him. The Indian had found a way down the cliff and now stood at the base of it. He held out his hand and Dolan shook it.

Lokan said something, and Whooper Bill interpreted. "He says thanks for you helping Scooter." The chief added something, and Whooper Bill said, "He says they've been watching F Ranch. When the crew rode out this morning,

he figured they was up to some deviltry, so the Injuns moved
along with 'em, keeping an eye on 'em. As soon as they
seen what Farrel was up to, they moved in to give us a
hand. He says they'll keep watching F Ranch."

"Thank him for us," Dolan said. "He saved our hides
today."

The chief listened gravely as Whooper Bill put it into
Paiute words. He was the first Paiute Dolan had ever seen
and was lighter skinned than he had expected. Taller, too,
so Dolan wondered if he was a Cheyenne or a member of
one of the other plains tribes who had drifted west and
joined the Paiutes.

Whatever Lokan was, he had the air of one who gave
orders and expected to be obeyed. Dolan remembered the
warning he had given Farrel the day he had saved Scooter
from the beating Larkin had started to give him, and how
Farrel had shrugged it off.

The chief extended his hand again, black eyes holding a
trace of amusement. Dolan gripped his hand, then Lokan
turned and made his way back up the slope in lithe, swift
movements. A few minutes later he disappeared over a
shoulder of Steens Mountain, the braves moving with him.

"An Injun never forgets an insult," Whooper Bill said. "I
don't care what kind of Injun he is. That fool Larkin should
of knowed better than to try layin' a hand on Scooter. But
Larkin don't have a lick of sense anyhow."

Dolan turned toward the wagons, the cold-stone feeling
in his belly giving way to one of watery weakness. Joel and
Bud were standing beside the middle wagon, their faces
showing their relief. Ruth remained under the east wagon,
but Sandy had crawled out from under it and ran to Dolan.
When she reached him, she threw her arms around him and
hugged him.

"I don't know why I let my mouth get me into trouble
with you all the time," she said. "I don't even know what I
thought you were going to do, but I never dreamed you'd
walk out there and make bullet bait out of yourself."

He hugged her, liking the soft feel of her body. He said,
"It wasn't a smart thing to do. I saw that after it was too
late."

Suddenly Sandy realized what was happening and
blushed. She jerked away, saying sharply, "I apologize for

being so forward. It's just that I guess I never came so close to getting killed before."

"You never will be again, either," he said, "until you are."

When they reached the wagons, Dolan said, "We'll be safe for a while, I think. As long as the Paiutes are here anyway, but they'll be heading into Nevada this fall. Then we'll have to do it over again."

"By that time we'll be ready for 'em," Joel said, "and maybe have the law on our side. Before we left Nebraska I seen one of the senators and told him what Farrel was doing and he promised to send a U.S. marshal in here to make Farrel take the fence down. He ain't got here, I reckon. Or Farrel got to him if he did come."

"Maybe he'll still get here," Dolan said.

He didn't believe it, and the idea that the law might be here by the time the Paiutes left seemed to him to be dreaming big.

CHAPTER 20

DOLAN SPENT the rest of the day fishing, and Bud and Whooper Bill rode up on a shoulder of Steens Mountain to cut juniper posts for a corral until suppertime. Joel puttered around camp, chopped wood, and then just sat and stared at the campfire.

After supper Joel seemed more like himself than he had since Lon's death. He said to Whooper Bill, "Is there some ranch around here where we could buy a small herd of heifers?"

"Yeah, just the other side of the Nevada line," Whooper Bill answered. "It's a purty good-sized outfit. Belongs to a man named McCall. He don't cotton to Farrel. If he knows you're bucking Bronc, he'll sell you all the heifers you can buy."

"We've got to hire some help," Joel said. "You know of anybody in the country who wants to work?"

"I ain't been to old man Hodig's new store," Whooper Bill said, "but there's a bunch of sodbusters who have settled in Horn Valley. Chances are some of 'em want work. Cash money is something most of 'em don't have."

"Want to take a pasear up there tomorrow, Rafe?" Joel asked. "Hire two or three men. We need a good cowhand and a feller to haul lumber, and later on we'll need a carpenter to build a house."

"Sure," Dolan said. "I've been thinking you'd better write another letter, Joel. I don't have much faith it'll work, but the county government won't be any help. If we ever get Farrel's fence down, it'll have to be Uncle Sam who does it."

Joel nodded. "Get out your pen and ink and paper,

Sandy," he said. "We'll write it now. Rafe can take the letter with him in the morning."

"You'd better ride with me," Dolan said to Whooper Bill. "I'm not sure I can find this Horn City that Hodig started."

"All right," Whooper Bill said. "I can ride there and back, I reckon."

They left in the morning before the sun showed over Steens Mountain. Before they had ridden fifty yards, Whooper Bill said, "You didn't fool me a little bit, Rafe. You could find Horn City, all right. You figured you might have some trouble when you rode past F Ranch. Or when you went through the fence. If there was, you wanted a good man siding you. That old Joel, why hell, he couldn't lick his weight in hummingbirds."

"Sure, I wanted a good man siding me," Dolan agreed, "but don't you try to find out how good Joel is. Just remember he's the one with the dinero."

"Oh, I ain't gonna forget that," Whooper Bill said.

The truth was Dolan didn't want to leave Whooper Bill behind him all day. It would be ridiculous and tragic if the two old men decided to find out which one was the better man.

Whooper Bill rode in silence for a mile before he said, "Rafe, you know as well as I do that Joel would never have got his wagons through the fence if it hadn't been for you. I want to know what you're fixing to do now. If you ride off and leave that old goat with his daughter-in-law and his two grandchildren, they'll all get beefed 'cause they ain't got sense enough to run. Bronc was right about being a patient man. You know what he'll do sooner or later."

Dolan didn't answer. He hadn't slept much during the night. Most of the time he had been fully awake thinking of this very thing. He had thrown in with Joel and his party to get at Bronc Farrel. He guessed he had never really thought past yesterday morning. The showdown had been postponed for weeks, perhaps months. The idea of staying at Antelope Spring and helping with the work that it would take to develop a ranch appalled him.

"Well?" Whooper Bill pressed. "You ain't answering my question."

"No, and I'm not going to," Dolan snapped. "Now shut up."

Whooper Bill chuckled. "Sure, I'll shut up, but you're trapped and I guess I'm trapped with you. You can't leave, and as long as you're here, I won't leave, neither. I guess I want to see Bronc brought down a peg or two as much as anybody, and I figure you're the man who can do it."

Dolan didn't say anything, but he thought glumly that the old buckaroo was right about being trapped. He wouldn't stay and he couldn't leave. This was the kind of situation he had managed to avoid all of his life, and he didn't know why he had got into this one. But he had done it by his own choice, and now he had no idea what to do.

They had no trouble as they rode past F Ranch or later when they went through the fence. Near noon Dolan saw a sign near the road in the sagebrush, HORN CITY. He smiled, deciding that old man Hodig had the most far-sighted vision of anyone he had ever heard of.

A few minutes later they reined up in front of the store and dismounted and tied. Dolan stood at the hitch pole for a moment, staring at the dusty street which had been cleared of sagebrush. According to the sign, this was Main Street.

A short distance to the north was another street named Lincoln Avenue. Half a dozen tents were strung out along Main Street, but the store was the only building. "For Sale" signs marked every lot on both streets, and as he turned into the store, Dolan couldn't help admiring old man Hodig for trying. Along with being farsighted, he was optimistic.

Whooper Bill had gone inside. As Dolan stepped through the door, he heard a shrill voice yell, "By grab, I ain't letting none o' Farrel's bastards come into my store. I done it once and I got hell beat out of me. Now you git."

"Put that scattergun up, Hodig," Whooper Bill said in disgust. "I'm on your side. I ain't working for Bronc no more."

"You're a liar," Hodig screamed. "You're the dangedest liar in Horn Valley, and I wouldn't believe a word you said if you had your hand on the first Bible writ by Moses his-self. Royce!" He waited a few seconds and yelled, "Royce, get in here and throw this old buzzard out."

Dolan quickly crossed the store to where Hodig stood

behind the counter, a cocked shotgun lined on Whooper Bill's belly. Dolan asked, "Are you Mr. Hodig?"

The storekeeper stared at him for a moment. He was a small man with a wispy moustache and beard and a very long nose. His hair was white and his parchment skin was cut by deep lines. His eyes were his most distinguishing feature, very dark eyes that glittered with rage. They were the eyes of a fanatic. Dolan remembered he had once seen a missionary to the Crows with eyes exactly like Hodig's.

"Nobody ever calls me mister," Hodig said. "I'm old man Hodig. I'm the father of Horn City, and I hate Bronc Farrel, and I'll kill him if I ever get a chance. I might even kill one of his men if I don't get a chance at Farrel hisself."

Dolan held out his hand. "I'm Rafe Dolan. I'm helping develop a ranch at Antelope Spring. We cut Farrel's fence near the gate." He jerked a thumb at Whooper Bill. "He wasn't lying. He's on our side."

Hodig blinked and shot a glance at a man who had come into the store from the saloon, which was a room next to the store. "This the feller you were telling me about, Royce?"

Dolan turned to see an F Ranch buckaroo named Jay Royce standing a few feet inside the store. The man stared at Dolan a moment and nodded. He said, "That's the jasper, all right. I only seen him once at the gate, but I sure heard plenty about him. I reckon he's the only man in the country wearing buckskins."

"Well, by dogies." Hodig held out a skinny hand. "I sure am pleased to meet the man who put Pete Larkin down."

Dolan had dropped his hand to his side, but he extended it again and gripped Hodig's. "There's a few more things you haven't heard," he said, and told Hodig about the fight at the gate and Farrel's attempt to run Joel and his party out of the country. "We're here to stay. I rode over to hire a couple of men if you know where I can find 'em, a cowhand and a man to haul lumber."

"I'm looking for a riding job," Royce said. "I didn't figure anybody in these parts would hire me, but I'll work for you if you'll take me."

"He's a good man," Whooper Bill said.

Royce was about forty, Dolan judged, with the bowed

legs and the sun-hammered face of a buckaroo. Dolan asked, "Why did you quit F Ranch?"

"I got a little sassy and Larkin beat hell out of me," Royce said. "I'd like to even the score with him. If you figure there'll be a little powder burned, I'm your man."

Dolan glanced at Whooper Bill, who nodded and said again, "He's a good man."

"All right," Dolan said. "You're hired. There'll be some powder burned, all right. You can count on it."

"There's a feller camped up the street who wants work," Hodig said. "Name of Saul Higgins. He's got a wife and passel o' kids. I think he'll haul lumber for you." He nodded at Royce. "Go fetch him so Dolan can get a look at him."

Dolan bought cheese and crackers, a can of sardines, and two cans of peaches. Dividing the food with Whooper Bill, he stood at the counter and ate while he listened to Hodig tell how Farrel and Willie Martin had come to his old store and Martin had beaten him until he had agreed to sell.

"They'd have killed me if I hadn't," Hodig said. "I had this building and I was figuring on moving over here later on, but I wasn't ready yet. I wanted to stay there for the summer and try to talk folks into going through the gate and following the county road, which they had a right to do, but Farrel didn't give me no choice, so here I am. A lot of people have moved into Horn Valley this summer, and I ain't gonna be satisfied till we get that fence down. Or the gate unlocked so anybody can travel the county road who wants to."

Dolan laid Joel's letter on the counter. "I've got a letter addressed to the Department of the Interior. It's from Joel Kendall, the man I work for. He's asking for a special agent to be sent here to make Farrel take his fence down."

"Well now," Hodig said, grinning. "I'll be dad-gummed if that ain't peculiar. There'll be a mail stage through here this evening, so that letter will go out today. One week from today when the mail stage comes back, there'll be an agent on it. Feller named Fred Berry. I had a letter telling me about it last week. You see, I've been firing letters to the Department of Interior as fast as I could and I finally got some action." Hodig cackled. "You can tell your boss that his letter was the one that done the trick."

Hodig pulled at his beard, scowling. "But then I don't expect no good to come from it. There's been special agents here before and nothing happened. Farrel always knows when they're coming and he gets to 'em first and gives 'em whisky and some good meals and takes 'em hunting and fishing. Bribes 'em, maybe, though nobody can prove that."

Hodig walked around the counter to stand beside Dolan. He waggled a skinny forefinger at him. "You see, the agents just get on the stage and leave, saying they'll do something about the fence, but they never do. If they did try to take some legal action, Farrel has got the dinero to hire the best lawyers on the coast, so he'd tied the case up for years. But, damn it, we've got to keep trying. I ain't sure how or when it'll happen, but someday the law's gonna come to this country."

Royce came in with another man and introduced him as Saul Higgins. He was big and square-shouldered with a firm handshake. About fifty, Dolan thought, with gray eyes that met Dolan's. Higgins said, "I want work. I can handle horses. I ain't afraid of Farrel and his tough hands if that worries you."

"You've got the job," Dolan said, instinctively liking the man.

Higgins turned to Hodig. "I don't know when I'll get home. You see that my wife gets whatever she needs."

"Don't you worry none, Saul," Hodig answered. He looked at Dolan and scratched an ear, and blurted, "I don't figure to tell you your business or this feller Kendall you say you're working for, but you can't stay down there at Antelope Spring and get anywhere. Even if the fence comes down, sooner or later Farrel will cook your goose."

"Got any ideas?"

"Yes," Hodig said. "Hire an army of gunfighters. In the end Farrel has got to be whipped. You can't settle this no other way."

Dolan nodded. "He's got to be whipped, all right, but who's got the money to hire 'em? Have you?"

"No," Hodig said gloomily. "I figured your boss Kendall did."

Dolan shook his head. "He's got too much else to pay for."

As he rode back to Antelope Spring later that afternoon, Dolan thought about what Hodig had said. He felt more tightly trapped than ever. He would have to do what the army of gunfighters should be hired to do, and that was not the way he had planned it.

CHAPTER 21

DOLAN GOT BACK to Antelope Spring in time for supper. He had ridden on ahead of the other three so Ruth and Sandy would know they had to cook for two more men. He told Joel what had happened, adding, "Hodig says Farrel always seems to know when a special agent is coming. He gets to them first, so the agent winds up not doing anything. It strikes me I'd better see this Fred Berry before Farrel does."

Joel nodded. "You do whatever you figure is necessary." He knocked his pipe out against his boot heel. "I never felt like this before, and I've had plenty of times when I came close to cashing in, but I've got a notion that I'm purty close to the end of the line. I'm worried about them. I ain't gonna live long enough to build this ranch. They're gonna have to do it."

He nodded at Bud, who had brought an armload of wood to the fire, then at Sandy, who was standing near the tailgate of the middle wagon slicing ham. "I guess I'll never get over Lon's death. Or get over blaming myself for it. But them things ain't important. What is important is leaving them kids to fight Farrel by themselves."

Whooper Bill had said almost the same thing that morning, and Dolan had thought about it off and on all day. Now he stared at Joel, thinking rebelliously that the old man was hoping he'd promise to stay here and look after them. He was tempted every time he thought of Sandy. He liked Bud, too, but damned if he was going to let himself be lured into making any promises.

"You're imagining things," he said, and turned away.

But he couldn't turn away from the hard fact that sooner or later Bronc Farrel and his men would come again, that if he rode off and left Sandy and Bud to whatever fate Farrel gave them, he would hate himself the rest of his life. He was in no way responsible for them being here, but they were here, and he had assumed at least part of the responsibility for their safety when he had contracted to work for Joel Kendall.

The following morning Joel, Bud, and Royce rode south to buy and drive back a herd of cattle. Higgins started north with one wagon to get a load of lumber from the sawmill in the Blue Mountains. Whooper Bill went back on the mountain to cut juniper posts.

Dolan fished until noon and returned to camp with six big cutthroats; he went hunting in the afternoon and brought in an antelope, but for some reason he felt little pride in what he had done. He was marking time. No more.

He was tempted to ride to F Ranch and force a fight with Bronc Farrel. He was still certain that there would be no peace until the man was broke or dead, and he could see little chance of Farrel going broke. No matter how much he thought about it, Dolan wasn't sure it was the right time to make a move. He would very likely get himself killed and not accomplish what he had set out to do.

The next day he rode up on Steens Mountain to hunt and ran into Lokan and some of his Paiutes. The chief gravely offered his hand and said in excellent English, "You will find deer higher on the mountain."

Dolan shook the Indian's hand, surprised to hear him speak English that was better than most white men used. He said, "I thought you didn't know English."

"I know it, but I don't use it unless I have to," the chief said. "You don't savvy Paiute, do you?"

"No." Dolan shook his head. "I know Shoshoni and Sioux, but not Paiute. I've never been in this country before."

"I'm Cheyenne," the Indian said. "At least that was what I was told, but I don't remember. I was raised by a missionary named Lokan. That's how I got my name and how I learned to speak English. I ran away before I was grown and a band of Paiutes took care of me." He stared across the desert, silent for a moment, a brooding expression coming into his bronze-skinned face, then he added, "Most white men are mean bastards. I know from experience. Not many of them would have interfered when Larkin was beating Scooter."

"Oh, I don't know—" Dolan began.

"I do," Lokan interrupted with some bitterness. "You're an Indian, at least in the way you think and the way you live. You don't like white men's ways any better than I do. You don't work. You hunt."

Dolan grinned and nodded agreement. "You're right. I guess I'm plain lazy. I don't like to work and that's a fact, but maybe I'm going to have to. The country's changing and I'll either change or move on."

"We should have killed Farrel and his men," Lokan said, the bitterness growing. "You will not be safe as long as he is alive."

"No, you'd have made outlaws out of yourselves if you had, and you would have been punished," Dolan said. "The army would have moved in and called it an outbreak."

"I know." The chief scowled. "We would have died for no reason just as thousands of Indians have died at the hands of whites."

"I keep thinking I ought to go to F Ranch and kill Farrel," Dolan said, "but I might run into his whole crew and get myself killed. That wouldn't do any good."

"No, it wouldn't," the chief agreed. "What you said about making outlaws out of ourselves is true. It's easy for any Indian to do that in white man's country. If we stay on the mountain, we can live in peace while we're here, but we'll be going south in about a month, and down there we can get into trouble without even looking for it."

Lokan turned his horse and rode downslope toward his camp without another word. Dolan worked his way up the mountain, angling back and forth, and twice dropping into deep gorges that carved the western side of Steens Mountain, but he returned to camp that evening without a deer.

The rest of the week he went with Whooper Bill to cut juniper posts, thinking that work might get his mind off the problems that faced him, but it didn't help. He didn't forget, either, that the federal agent, Fred Berry, was coming in on the next stage.

Near the end of the week he asked Whooper Bill, "You know the country the mail stage comes through?"

"Yeah, I've been all over it," Whooper Bill said. "We ran some cattle over there the second year Bronc was here and I spent the summer at the cow camp. Why?"

"What's it like?"

"It's just a sagebrush flat for a ways out of Horn City," Whooper Bill answered, "then you get into some foothills that's purty well covered by junipers. A little farther on where it gets higher there's some good pines."

"We're going there in the morning," Dolan said. "Just you'n me."

"What for?" the old buckaroo asked. "I've told you I don't ride worth a damn no more."

"You can ride that far," Dolan said. "We're stopping the stage and taking Fred Berry off it. I aim to be sure I'm the first man who talks to him."

"Oh no, not me," Whooper Bill said uneasily. "I ain't doing no such thing. If you want the law after you, all right, but not me."

"What law are you talking about?" Dolan asked. "And can you think of any other way to get to Fred Berry before Farrel does? Chances are he'll be right there at Hodig's store just waiting for Berry to get off the stage."

"Yeah, I reckon he will be," Whooper Bill admitted, "but holding up a stage and kidnapping a Federal agent—" He shook his head. "That's all it would take to get us an inside view of a federal prison."

"Maybe that's one way to get the law to come to this country," Dolan said.

Joel, Bud, and Royce brought the cattle in that night and left them to graze in the grassy meadow across the creek. "We'll use NK for our brand," Joel said. "Lon's initials. I don't aim to let him be forgot."

"He won't be," Bud said. "We'll see to that."

Dolan didn't tell Joel what he intended to do. After supper he said he was going to be gone for a day or two and Whooper Bill was going with him. Joel looked at him anxiously and asked, "You're coming back?"

This was the way it would be, Dolan thought. He was reminded again more forcibly the next morning when he saddled his horse. He heard Sandy call and turned to see her running toward him. When she reached him, she said, "Grandpa told me you'd be gone for a while. He didn't know what you were going to do or where you were going."

"I didn't tell him," Dolan said. "I'm not going to tell you, either."

She tipped her head back and looked at him, the early morning sunlight falling on one side of her face. "I'm worried, Rafe. Be careful." She swallowed. "Farrel knows how important to us you are, but I'm not sure you do."

"I guess he does," Dolan agreed, "and I guess I don't. So long."

She hesitated, her eyes still on his face, then suddenly she leaned forward and kissed him on the cheek, whirled, and ran back to the fire. He mounted and rode north, Whooper Bill reining in beside him.

"I don't know why I'm here," the old buckaroo grumbled. "I told you I wasn't going."

"I guess you did say something like that," Dolan said.

"You're gonna get your face plumb dirty on that one side where she kissed you," Whooper Bill said, "on account of I don't suppose you'll ever wash it."

Dolan didn't say anything, so Whooper Bill, emboldened by his silence, went on, "That gal sure is in love with you. What are you gonna do about it?"

Dolan turned his head and said, "By God, you're sticking your knife into me too many times. I've had enough of it. If you keep on, I'll pull you out of your saddle and clean your plow for you good."

"Oh, you could do it easy enough," Whooper Bill said. "It strikes me you're purty damn cranky. I figure we're gonna have to go after Farrel. If we don't, we're stuck here and that girl is gonna have you roped and tied."

"You got any kick about that?"

"No," Whooper Bill admitted, "except that you've always said you'd never let yourself get saddled with a wife and kids. I figured you'd be riding off one of these days and I'd ride with you. I guess I don't want to stay in this country after all."

Dolan let it drop, but he told himself a man could have a worse fate than to be roped and tied by Sandy Kendall. In spite of his mental protests about staying he wondered if Sandy wasn't part of what had held him this long. Sandy was in love with him. He was sure of that, and it was a very pleasant thought, the first time in his life when he had even dreamed of a white woman feeling that way about him.

When they reached the fence, Dolan saw that it had been repaired, but the gate was open. Two buckaroos stood in front of the small tent, their Winchesters on the ready. They were watching him closely as if trying to guess what he was going to do.

"Got any kick about us going through the gate?" Dolan called.

"Not one damned bit," one of the men answered. "For right now the boss said not to stop any of your outfit from going through, but nobody else." The buckaroo tongued his quid of tobacco to the other side of his mouth, spat at the nearest clump of sagebrush, and added, "I don't look for him to let your bunch through after today."

"We'll see," Dolan said, and rode through the gate, wondering if they'd have to fight their way through again.

They reached Horn City about noon and dismounted. They watered their horses, Dolan saying, "We'll buy some grub and get moving. We'll get there in time, won't we?"

"Sure," Whooper Bill said. "It ain't far from here, and the stage don't get here till evening."

They tied their mounts and went into the store, Whooper Bill in the lead. He took three steps into the big room and no more. A man lunged forward from where he had been standing against the wall and struck him a vicious blow across the top of his head. Whooper Bill's knees folded and he sprawled on the floor.

Dolan had made one step past the door when Whooper Bill went down. He clawed for his gun butt, gripped it and had the barrel half out of leather when a second man jabbed him in the side with the muzzle of his revolver.

"Hoist 'em, Dolan," the man said. "I want to shoot you in the guts. Give me an excuse and I will."

Dolan recognized the voice. Without turning his head to look, he knew the man was Willie Martin.

CHAPTER 22

JOEL STOOD beside the campfire watching Dolan and Whooper Bill ride north until they disappeared over the ridge. Sandy had carried a bucket of water from the creek. Now she set it down, asking, "What's he up to, Grandpa?"

"He's aiming to get at this federal agent who's coming in on the stage today," Joel answered, "but I dunno how he's gonna work it."

"Is he going to stay here with us?"

"I dunno about that, neither," Joel said. "He's never stayed long enough in any place to take root. Sometimes I think he's more Indian than white man. It's in his blood, wanting to drift and live off the land and be a free man. I ain't real sure he can settle down any place long enough to take root."

"I know," she said sadly. "I think he's afraid of white women. I guess he's been around Indian squaws too long."

Joel gave her a sharp glance. "You think a lot of him, don't you?"

"Yes." She laughed, mocking herself. "I never thought I would say that. When you introduced him to us there at Martin's store, I thought he was some sort of relic from the past. A phony wearing those clothes, but he's not a phony. I guess he's the bravest man I ever met."

"He's sure the toughest," Joel said. "He's a killer, too. He wasn't when I knew him, but he was a boy then. He's a man now. When we had that fight at the gate, he used his revolver like a Gatling gun. I never seen anything like it."

"He's not just a tough killer," Sandy said. "You watch his face sometime. I did when we were burying Pa. He's got a gentle side. He could love a woman if he'd let himself." She paused, thinking about it, then added, "Maybe he's afraid to risk loving someone. It is a risk, you know. Suppose you love someone who doesn't love you?"

Joel nodded. He turned the idea over in his mind. It had never occurred to him before. Then his thoughts swung to Lon as they did so often. He wondered if Lon had died thinking that no one in the whole world loved him except Ruth, that everyone else in his family had only contempt for him.

Joel could not bear to keep thinking about Lon. He took out his pipe and filled and lighted it, watching Sandy, who did nearly all of the work. Her mother sat in a rocking chair near the back wheel of a wagon, the only one that still had its bows and sheet and held the load of freight that it had hauled from Nebraska.

The other two wagons had been unloaded. Higgins used one to bring lumber from the sawmill to the north, and Bud was hooking up the second one to go after a load of corral posts on the mountain.

Joel didn't understand Ruth. He never had, but he understood her less than ever now. She had been a wild woman the day Lon was killed, blaming Joel for it and telling him and Sandy and Bud that Lon had known what they thought of him. She had seen to it that Lon was properly buried and had read at his grave, and after that she had been her old self again.

No, not exactly her old self because she had done her share of the camp chores after they had left Nebraska. Now she didn't seem to want to do anything. She never talked unless spoken to, and then sometimes not until she was spoken to twice. She would sit all day in the rocking chair and stare unseeingly at the desert to the west or the mountain to the east, and act as if she were in some kind of a daze. Maybe she was. Joel didn't know whether she was or not. At least she wasn't hating him. He guessed she wasn't feeling anything. She was just numb, and he wasn't sure she would ever be any different.

Joel wheeled away from the fire and strode to his roan gelding that had been staked near the creek. He saddled him, knowing he had to get away from here. He didn't know where he would go. He didn't much care. He just had to get away from Ruth and Lon's grave.

He rode west, nodding to Jay Royce, who was cutting

willows along the creek. The sooner they got at least one corral built the better. Royce was a good man. He wasn't much of a talker, but he was willing to work, and that, Joel knew, was more than he could say for most cowboys. Royce seemed to understand that some things had to be done to start a working ranch. Apparently he wanted to stay here, so he was willing to do whatever work was necessary.

Joel put his horse through the creek and crossed the grass-covered meadow to the west. The cattle they had brought up from Nevada were scattered here. Farther downstream the grass was higher and could be cut for hay in a few days. He had brought Lon's mower in one of the wagons, but he didn't have a rake. Maybe Hodig had one at his store. He'd tell Dolan to ask the next time he was there.

He was in the sagebrush now, riding toward the distant rimrock that made a faint line ahead of him through the haze. No reason for him to ride this way. He had just let his horse pick his direction. He glanced up at the sky. Clear. Not even a cottony cloud on the horizon.

There had been no rain since that first night, and that had been only a sprinkle. He took a long breath, and in spite of his decision not to think about Lon's death, he found his thoughts returning to the gate and Lon's murder. He could not keep those events out of his mind.

The truth was he had been in agony from the terrible moment Lon had stepped down from the wagon seat and had carried the clippers to the fence and had cut the top wire. He had not understood then why Lon had done it. He still didn't. It just hadn't been like Lon. Bud, yes, but not Lon. Maybe he had done it to keep Bud from cutting the wire. Joel had not thought of that before, but it was about the only explanation that made any sense.

It had been a mistake to bring Lon and his family out here. Joel knew that, now that it was too late to change what had happened. He should have used his money to build a decent house on the Nebraska farm where Ruth and Lon had wanted to live. He should have paid off the mortgage and bought a good team and some farm equipment and let Lon and Ruth stay there and rot.

Oh, he had known that Lon wouldn't make a good living if he had stayed in Nebraska, but he should have let him stay anyhow. No matter how much Ruth knifed Joel about thinking Lon was a failure, he had been a failure and there was no use trying to cover it up.

Bringing Lon out here had not changed anything except that the new, raw country had panicked him and had taken from him even his desire to live. Thinking about it now as he had every day since Lon's death, Joel had finally come to the conclusion that Lon would have killed himself if a bullet from one of Farrel's men hadn't.

Lon had been a sick man, knowing he could not face life on the frontier and knowing too that Rafe Dolan was a man who could. Perhaps he had compared himself to Dolan and had realized then how far he was from filling the bill.

Joel had never been a man to worry about the past. Or the future, either. He'd proved to himself over and over that he could meet any emergency that came his way. If something turned out wrong, he went on to whatever had to be done next, dead certain in his mind that it wouldn't turn out wrong again.

Dolan had been right about him torturing himself, but Joel had kept right on doing it. As he thought back over these last weeks from the time he had ridden up to Lon's sod house and told him they were all moving out to Oregon, he realized he had never let Lon decide anything. That much of what Ruth had said was true. He guessed that just about all she had said was true when you came right down to it.

The future was different. It concerned Sandy and Bud. He was like Dolan in the sense that he had never taken time to learn to love anyone. Maybe, as Sandy had said, he had been afraid to risk love. His life had been one of action; he had been able to do many things and do them well.

Life would be different from now on. During this trip he had learned to love Sandy and Bud. They were the finest kind of kids and he told himself for their sake he was glad he had done what he had. They had no chance to get ahead in Nebraska. Out here they could. But everything depended on Rafe Dolan. The bitter truth was that he, Joel Kendall, was no longer sure he could meet the emergencies that came his way.

Now he faced the equally bitter truth that if Rafe left, the ranch would fail. Old Whooper Bill would ride away with him. Jay Royce would be afraid to stay. Higgins would feel the same way and return to his wife and children in

Horn City. Rafe Dolan had a way of giving strength and courage to other men. Give Bud a chance to become a man and he would be a good one, but he needed time.

Joel turned his roan and headed back to Antelope Spring. He glanced at the sun. It was almost noon. He had ridden farther than he had intended. He'd get into camp late for dinner and Sandy would needle him about it and claim he was making her a lot of extra work. All he could say was that he was sorry and that was a hell of a poor thing to say. He'd been saying he was sorry about Lon's death ever since the shooting and it hadn't helped a damned bit.

He saw a rider ahead of him a long time before they met. At first the other man was just a moving dot on the desert, angling south, maybe from F Ranch, though he wasn't sure of that. At first he thought they were not going to meet, then he realized that the rider had changed his course and was heading straight toward him.

Joel had never been afraid of anything. Actually he hadn't thought about it because he'd expected to handle any trouble that came to him. Rafe Dolan was the same. It was an attitude that stemmed from the way a man lived.

The ones who were afraid stayed home; the ones who were reckless or not capable of coping with the dangers of the frontier died early. If he was meeting a dozen men and judged they were F Ranch hands, Joel would have started looking for some place to hole up, but he figured he was as good as any one man Bronc Farrel had, so he rode toward the rider, who was still riding straight at him.

It was another fifteen minutes before they met. The man was forking a black gelding. When they were twenty yards apart, he saw the fellow's fancy calfskin vest and the bristling yellow moustache and knew who the man was. He was Pete Larkin, the F Ranch ramrod who had reason to hate Rafe Dolan.

Suddenly Joel was aware that Larkin's right hand hung at his side and was not visible; he remembered some of the things Dolan had told him about Larkin, and he knew, in that one sharp moment of insight, that he should have been holding his revolver in his hand.

Joel went for his gun, his memory very sharp in this one tense moment as he whipped his gun out of leather. He had told Dolan only last night that he had a feeling he was close to the end of the line. This was the end of the line. He knew it even as the barrel of his Colt came level.

He was just a trifle slow. Larkin's gun swept up and leveled and went off, and Joel was slammed back by the impact of the heavy slug. He tried desperately to hold his gun level, to fire it, but he could not. He glimpsed Larkin's leering, triumphant face, then he was falling into space, pinwheeling head over heels down and down into a black tunnel that had no bottom. He didn't feel anything when he hit the ground.

Larkin laughed as he stepped out of his saddle. Frightened, Kendall's horse pranced away nervously, but became quiet and stood motionless as Larkin spoke to him. He patted the animal on the neck, saying, "The old boy didn't figure out who I was until it was too late. One less gun when we clean out that rat nest."

He lifted Joel's body in to the saddle and laid him belly down across it, then an afterthought struck him and he fished around in his pockets until he found a scrap of paper and a stubby pencil. He wrote: GET OUT F then eased the body back and slipped the paper into Joel's shirt pocket.

He took Joel's rope down, lashed the body into place, and mounted. For several miles he led the roan toward Antelope Spring, then looped the reins around the saddle horn and gave the animal a clout on the rump with his hat.

The horse would wind up back in camp sooner or later. Larkin laughed again as he reined north toward F Ranch, thinking how Dolan would cuss his head off when he saw the old man's body. Then his face turned grave as he thought about Bronc Farrel, who kept saying, "No hurry. We'll clean them out when the time's right."

The time was right now, but he wasn't sure Farrel could be convinced. Pete Larkin had not had a good night's sleep from the day Dolan had whipped him the first time they had met at Antelope Spring, and he wouldn't sleep until Rafe Dolan was dead.

CHAPTER 23

THE INSTANT Dolan felt the muzzle of Martin's revolver prodding him in the side, he knew that if he did anything, he had to do it then. Martin was slow of thought and therefore slow of action. He wanted to find an excuse to kill Dolan, and he would certainly find it if Dolan waited.

Dolan did the only thing he could, and the one thing Martin did not expect. He literally exploded in a lightning response; he made a quarter turn as his left arm knocked the barrel of Martin's gun to one side. Martin fired instinctively, but by the time he pulled the trigger, the gun was angled far enough to one side so that the bullet sliced through Dolan's buckskin shirt without touching him.

Dolan lowered his shoulders and lunged forward, the top of his skull catching Martin squarely on the chin, cracking his head hard against the wall. Dolan brought his right fist through to Martin's belly, hammering breath out of his lungs.

One of the other men fired, the slug thwacking into the wall an inch or so from Dolan's head. That was the only clear shot the man had. Dolan grabbed Martin by the shoulder and whirled him around in front of him so that his big body was an adequate shield. At the same time Dolan's left arm swept up and circled Martin's throat.

Dolan choked the F Ranch man as he reached for his revolver; he heard the roar of a shotgun and saw one of the men go down, his head battered into blood pulp. Then Dolan had his revolver in his hand and he fired at the second man who had been trying to throw a shot at Dolan without hitting Martin. The buckaroo fell back against the counter. He hung there for a moment, draped across it like a rag doll, then his feet slid out from under him and he fell to the floor.

Martin had momentarily been knocked out, or close to it, but now he kicked and squirmed and dug at Dolan with his elbows, but Dolan tightened his grip on the man's throat until he went limp, and would have fallen if Dolan had not supported him.

Dolan loosened his hold on the man's throat so he could breathe, his gaze sweeping the room. The two buckaroos were on the floor, dead or close to it, and Hodig, who had accounted for one of them, still held the smoking shotgun in his hand. It was double-barreled, so he still had one load he didn't need.

"Watch those two bastards in case one of 'em can still get at his iron," Dolan yelled.

Martin had begun to buck and kick again. Dolan dragged him through the door and on to the horse trough; he jammed his face into the water and held it there. Martin kicked and lunged harder than ever, but Dolan kept his nose and mouth in the water until the man quit struggling, then he yanked him back and let him drop into the mud around the trough.

Martin lay on his back, his mouth sagging open as he struggled for breath, his eyes glassy. Dolan looked down at him in disgust. "You like a sure thing, don't you? You had your three friends hide inside the tent the other day at the gate so they could dry-gulch us, and this time you stay inside the store until we come in. I'm surprised you didn't smoke us down before we got to the door."

Martin made no attempt to say anything. He sat up, coughing and spitting and retching. Dolan said, "I guess you couldn't pass up a chance to have some fun with us, could you? You wanted us to know you were going to beef us and maybe you figured on making Whooper Bill crawl before you did it. Right now you look like a fish out of water. I guess I'll put you back in it."

Now Martin did try to say something, but the sounds he made were not words. He was begging for his life, Dolan thought as he turned away. No matter what Willie Martin deserved, Dolan could not murder him in cold blood.

He strode into the store and got a good look at the man Hodig had shot. He muttered, "My God, Hodig, you made sausage out of the man's head."

"That I did," Hodig said grimly. "I should have shot 'em as they came through the door. I've got two scatterguns.

One of 'em was hid under the counter. When they found the other one, they figgered they'd pulled my fangs. They were here to meet the stage and rode in early to do some drinking. They were fixing to hooraw me while they done it. They aimed to take Fred Berry out to F Ranch. Like I told you, Farrel always gets to these agents first."

Whooper Bill lay on the floor where he had fallen, still out cold. The man Dolan shot was dead, the bullet hitting him almost in the center of his chest. Dolan picked the old buckaroo up, saying, "He's hurt pretty bad, Hodig. Where's your bed?"

Hodig jerked a thumb toward the door. "Through there."

Dolan carried the old man into the bedroom and laid him on the bed. For a moment he stood staring down at Whooper Bill, wondering how hard he had been hit. In any case, he would not be going on to wait for the stage with Dolan. Dolan doubted that he could even sit his saddle for several days. He wheeled and strode out of the bedroom and through the store to the street.

Martin was on his feet, one hand clutching the end of the horse trough. His face was very pale as he swayed back and forth like a stalk of grass in the wind.

Dolan saw that Hodig had followed him outside. He said, "Willie looks a mite puny, don't he, Hodig?"

"Maybe he'll stay away from here after this," Hodig said. "Next time I'll start shooting the minute I see him coming. You know, they didn't figure on you and Whooper Bill showing up, but one of 'em had been outside and seen who you were when you were still down the road a piece. They got to talking about how they'd hooraw you awhile before they beefed you. They laughed their stinking heads off thinking about all the things they was going to do."

"Funny, wasn't it?" Dolan asked, jabbing a fist into Martin's belly. "I guess I'll get a rope and put it on your neck and drag you back to F Ranch for Farrel to look at." He turned to Hodig. "Where's their horses?"

"They're in the corral yonder," Hodig said. "They pulled off their saddles, figuring they'd be here till evening when the stage got in."

"I'll put the saddles back on," Dolan said, "and then we'll let him take those two pieces of carrion to F Ranch. I'm curious about what Farrel will say. He gave Martin a simple chore and he winds up getting two men killed and almost drowning himself. It ought to be a tolerable interesting conversation."

"No," Martin said. "I won't take 'em back."

"Chances are Farrel will kill him," Hodig said.

"Maybe you'd rather have me drag you awhile behind my horse," Dolan said. "It's that or take the carcasses back for Farrel to see."

Martin swallowed and coughed and swallowed again. He said, "All right, I'll take 'em."

Dolan saddled the three horses and led them to the water trough. "Get aboard, Martin," he said. "I'll carry the bodies out here and tie them on their horses. You tell Farrel to let us alone or we'll come after him."

Martin, still pale, lurched to his horse and stood beside him for a moment, both hands gripped the saddle horn. By the time Dolan had brought the bodies from the store and tied them across the saddles, Martin had laboriously pulled himself into the saddle.

"Get moving," Dolan said. "Tell Farrel he don't have to bother meeting the stage. I'll do it."

Martin rode away, leading the horses that carried the dead men. Hodig, staring thoughtfully at Martin's back, said, "I'll give you two-to-one odds that he never goes to F Ranch."

"I won't take that bet," Dolan said. "It's a loser. I had the same notion myself. He'll go part way and head those horses toward F Ranch and then he'll get out of the valley and stay out. I think we busted him pretty good this time."

"How much farther will Farrel go?"

"All the way," Dolan answered. "He's no Willie Martin. He can't turn back and he can't admit he's whipped. He can't stop until I'm dead and he's chased Joel Kendall and his family off what he claims is his range."

Hodig nodded grimly. "And he'll come visiting me again after he sees them carcasses. He won't let that go."

"I'm going to go sit with Whooper Bill awhile," Dolan said. "He took one hell of a crack on the noggin."

"I'll fix you some dinner," Hodig said. "I put some stew on the stove early this morning. It oughtta be done by now."

Whooper Bill still had not come around by the time Hodig brought a dish of stew, biscuits, and coffee to the bedroom. He said, "Dolan, maybe you haven't thought about it, but there ain't much sense in you meeting the stage. Farrel ain't gonna be here or send anyone else to talk to Fred Berry. Chances are he won't have time to get here before the stage does. It'll be up to me to tell Berry how Farrel operates."

"What do you think Farrel will be doing the rest of the afternoon and evening?" Dolan asked.

"He'll start looking for you as soon as he finds out what happened," Hodig said. "Looks to me like you'd better head out for Antelope Spring. Don't take the road, either. They'll be looking for you and they'll either haul you in to have a talk with Farrel or shoot you out of the saddle. It's all right for you to be filled with guts and hellfire, but if you get yourself killed, your friends at Antelope Spring will be left in one hell of a fix."

The old storekeeper paused, then said somberly, "Me, too, I reckon. I never knew Bronc Farrel to be afraid of anybody, but he never had to buck nobody like you before neither, so stay alive, damn it."

Dolan had been thinking about it as he'd sat here beside Whooper Bill. It was about all he had thought about for several days. He had never before been caught in such a bog of indecision, but he knew Hodig was right. Every time his mind lingered on Sandy, he realized he couldn't leave now and he couldn't take any long-odds risk getting killed, either.

Dolan finished eating, then asked, "How am I supposed to go back if I don't take the road?"

"Ride south from here and swing a mite to the west to get around the lakes," Hodig said, "then angle southeast after you've passed 'em, and you'll hit Steens Mountain close to Antelope Spring. It'll be farther that way and you'll have to take off through the sagebrush, but you oughtta make it before dark."

Whooper Bill was beginning to stir. He tried to talk, but the sounds he made were grunts and groans. Dolan said, "You're staying here at the store, Bill. Hodig will look after you. Stay in bed." He turned to the storekeeper. "Keep him flat on his back. His skull may be cracked for all we know. Since there's no doctor to look after him, you'll have to make him be careful or he may stand up and fall over dead."

"He's a stubborn old booger," Hodig said, "but I'll do all I can for him. I'll go take care of his horse. You'd better get started."

Dolan nodded and left the store. He had never been a patient man, and now, riding south, he told himself the waiting was over. It was time to go after Farrel.

CHAPTER 24

DOLAN REACHED camp as the last of the twilight was turning into night. He reined up, seeing Sandy and Bud run toward him from the campfire, and sensed at once that something was wrong.

He stepped down. The next instant they were there, Sandy gripping his arms as she said in a low tone, "Grandpa's dead, Rafe. They murdered him."

"Joel dead?" Dolan asked needlessly.

Somehow Joel Kendall had always seemed immortal to Dolan. Sandy began to cry and Dolan put his arms around her and drew her to him. She pressed her face against his shirt and seemed content to remain in that position. She needed him and he gave no thought beyond that.

Bud said tonelessly, "He's dead, all right. He left this morning just to take a ride, I guess. His horse came in early in the afternoon. Grandpa had been shot and his body was tied face down across his saddle."

"Did he still have his gun?"

"No, I don't know what happened to it," Bud answered. "I don't know where they killed him or who did it except there was a note in his pocket for us to git. There was an F at the bottom."

It didn't make much difference who did the actual shooting, Dolan thought. Pete Larkin might have killed him. Or Bronc Farrel. Or any of the F Ranch hands. If he had simply been out riding, somebody from F Ranch had run into him. They had quarreled and fought, or he might have just been shot out of his saddle.

This was murder as far as Dolan was concerned, and the need to square accounts for Joel Kendall simply confirmed his decision to go after Farrel tonight. There was still the chance he would run into the F Ranch crew, but now the situation had changed enough to make him take a chance.

"I'm going to F Ranch tonight," Dolan said. "You want to go, Bud?"

"Of course I want to go," the boy said passionately. "You couldn't make me stay home."

"One thing," Dolan said. "This is my game, not yours. In another five years it might be yours, too, but not tonight. I'll play it my way and you'll obey orders."

"Sure," Bud said, "but I'm going."

"You'll want your supper," Sandy said. "There's somebody here to see you. She's in our tent. I guess she's asleep now. I haven't talked to her for an hour or more."

It would be Liz Farrel, of course. He was not surprised. He had expected her to come before this. The only thing he was curious about was what had triggered her action today. She had faced an impossible situation for weeks, perhaps months, but there had been no place for her to go until now.

He had told her he wouldn't bring her here because it would give Farrel an excuse to attack the camp, but she had come anyway. She could have come yesterday or the day before or the day before that. Something must have happened today that had driven her off F Ranch.

The flap of the tent was thrown back. He went in and hunkered down beside her bed. He said, "I'm here, Liz."

She turned her head on the pillow and looked at him for a moment. In the thin light he saw that her face was pale, and in that instant he caught a glimpse of the despair that was in her. He sensed that she was not her old aggressive self. The fight had been beaten out of her. He had thought that wasn't possible.

"I was hoping nothing had happened to you," she said. "You were late getting in. Something did happen, didn't it? I know Bronc sent Willie Martin and a couple of other buckaroos to Hodig's store and Sandy said that was where you and Whooper Bill Munk were going."

He told her what had happened and how he had returned to camp, avoiding the road. He finished with, "I'd have got home sooner if I'd followed the road. Maybe I could have tracked Joel's killer if I had, so I've got a hunch I should have come by the road."

"No, it was a good thing you did what you did," she said.

"Willie never showed up at F Ranch, but one of the men at the gate saw the horses with the two dead men, so he brought them to Bronc. I never saw him as mad as he was then. He boiled over and cursed like a crazy man. He was going to get you, he said, and when he did, he'd kill you by inches. He sent every man he had at the ranch to hunt for you. If you had followed the road, you'd have run into the whole outfit and you'd be dead."

"Has he said anything about attacking the camp?"

"He's afraid to as long as the Indians are around here," she said. "He's the kind of gambler who makes his bets when the odds are on his side. Larkin has been after him to wipe your people out, but Bronc keeps saying there is plenty of time."

"Maybe he'll change his mind now and come after us."

"I don't think so," she said, "although he knows Joel Kendall is dead and that means one less rifle here. Larkin is the one who killed him. Larkin rode in just after Bronc heard about the men you'd killed. When he told Bronc about shooting Kendall and that it was time to attack your camp, Bronc told him to get to hell out of there. I guess Larkin had never seen Bronc so crazy mad. He's always been a little afraid of Bronc, I think. Anyhow, he rode off with the men to hunt you."

"What makes Bronc so sure I shot those men?"

"He says nobody else could have done it. He says you're a devil from hell and you've come here to haunt him. He hates you because you wouldn't keep on working for him, and then you made it worse when you came back with these people and settled on part of what he claims is his range. Sometimes he just sits and stares into space and broods about what he'll do when he decides it's time to make his move."

She paused, her gaze not leaving his face. She was not the same woman who had fed him that noon when he had stopped at F Ranch, or who had met him the first night he had ridden fence.

"Bronc has always been able to ride over any man who stood up to him," she went on. "You're the first one who's been tough enough to fight back and not get ridden down. Now you've got him buffaloed and he doesn't know what to do." She reached out and took his hands. "I don't understand you, either. You're the only man I ever wanted and the only man I couldn't have. Why?"

"I'm not the average man," he said.

"I knew that the first time I saw you," she said. "Maybe that was why you attracted me." She paused, still staring at him as if trying to read his face, then asked slowly, "This girl—Sandy—is she the one?"

"She's the one," he said, and was surprised at the ease with which he answered her. "Why are you in bed? Are you hurt?"

"Yes. Bronc came into the house after Larkin and the men left to hunt you. He accused me of being a—a bad woman and called me a lot of names and said all I wanted to do was to punish him for bringing me here. We had the worst fight we ever had. I got a horse and came here and fainted. Sandy put me to bed."

"How did he hurt you? Did he hit you?"

"Yes, but that wasn't the way he hurt me," she said. "What he said was mostly true. I'm a bad woman by his lights and I did everything I could to punish him. He lied to me when he married me and brought me here. He made a prisoner out of me and I got to hating him, so I hit back at him by giving myself to every man I could."

"You haven't answered my question. How did he hurt you?"

She turned her head so he couldn't see her face. She said, "You wouldn't understand."

"I might. Tell me."

"When he came into the house this afternoon after the men left," she said, "he wanted me to go to bed with him. I wouldn't do it. I had never turned him down before, but we hated each other so much I had made up my mind I was never going to bed with him again. When I said no, he hit me. He got me into bed and tore my clothes off and that was when he hurt me. Later I picked up a chamber pot and hit him on the head as hard as I could. It broke and I knocked him out. That was when I got my horse and left."

He rose and looked down at her, not sure it was the truth. She wouldn't be above lying to him to get his sympathy. Bronc Farrel did not seem like the kind of man who would rape his wife, but he might have been out of his mind with rage and therefore would have been capable of doing anything. The chances were, Dolan thought, he would never be sure what had happened.

"I'm sorry," he said.

"Don't feel sorry for me," she said. "I'll be all right in a day or two, but I'll never go back to him."

"We're riding to F Ranch," Dolan said. "Did he tell his men to come back tonight?"

"I don't think so," she said. "I mean, I don't believe they will. I know they were scared of Farrel when they left, so I don't think they'll come back until they know for sure where you are. Maybe they'll stay at the store and go on south the way you did as soon as it's daylight. Larkin will come back. That was the last thing he said before he rode off with the crew."

"Why would he come back?"

"If they didn't find you by dark, he thought you'd have gone back to the spring some other way. He was going after you, he said. Bronc didn't argue. He just said to move out."

Dolan considered this for a moment, still not sure she was telling the truth. It was unbelievable that Larkin would come alone to attack the camp, but no man was predictable when he reached a certain point of frustration. Larkin might do it, and if he hid out on the ridge to the north, he could shoot the camp to pieces as soon as it was daylight and be gone before the Indians heard the firing and had time to get here.

"I'll go eat supper," he said.

He left the tent and walked to the fire. Sandy said, "It's ready," and poured his coffee.

He hunkered by the fire and ate, turning the situation over in his mind. He had a hunch Liz was right about the crew staying at Hodig's store and following his tracks when it was daylight. He didn't worry much about them. If Farrel and Larkin weren't with them, the men wouldn't push too hard because they didn't have Farrel's and Larkin's deep feelings about people who settled on F Ranch range.

The men would track him here in time and then would probably go back to F Ranch for further instruction, but Larkin and Farrel were more uncertain. In any case, they wouldn't be here until dawn, and by that time it would be settled.

Royce and Higgins sat on the other side of the fire, their eyes on him. Bud had saddled his horse and stood waiting at the edge of the firelight. Ruth Kendall rocked back and forth, the chair making a shrill, squeaking sound. Sandy sat on the ground beside Dolan, motionless as she watched him, her long legs tucked under her.

Dolan put his empty plate down and finished his coffee. He set the tin cup beside the plate and said, "Royce, Bud and I are going to F Ranch. We need you, but it's up to you whether you ride with us or not."

"I'll go," Royce said.

"Good." Dolan rose as Royce left the fire to get his horse. "Higgins, you stay close to camp till we get back. I don't look for any trouble, but I don't want to leave the women without a man being here. If Farrel's crew shows up, tell them I'm not here. I'm at F Ranch. They won't stay when they find that out."

"I'll be here," Higgins said.

Dolan turned toward his horse, then stopped and wheeled back to face Sandy. A number of things had come clear. Maybe they had been clear before, but he had not been able to see them because he had been looking at the future as if it would go on being the same as his past, and now, with Joel Kendall dead, he was forced to admit at last that from now on everything would be different for Rafe Dolan.

For one thing, he knew he was staying. He guessed he had known all the time he would when the time came for him to make a decision, but there had been a choice as long as Joel was alive. Now he had no choice and he didn't fool himself any longer that he did.

Too, he had lived exactly as he had wanted to live, without restraints on his personal liberty. When a man marries and settles down, he accepts restraints. That was the reason Dolan had never given a white woman a second look. But Sandy was different and he had known that all along.

There was a crazy kind of humor in this, he told himself. He had hated cattlemen, but if he lived until morning, he could start planning his life as a cowman. He could think about working, too. He, Rafe Dolan, who had said he would never build a fence or plow a field, would be doing both and more.

Sandy was on her feet, waiting. He walked back to her

and put his arms around her and hugged her. He said,
"When the right time comes, I guess almost any man is willing to make some changes in his life. I've got some things
to say, but they'll wait."

"I want to hear them," she said, and swallowed, and then
her arms tightened their grip around him as if she would
not let him go, and whispered, "Rafe, have you got to do
this?"

"Yes," he said.

He kissed her. It was not a long kiss, but it was a good
kiss, filled with promise. He turned away and strode into
the darkness.

CHAPTER 25

THERE WAS NO moon and Dolan knew there would not be one tonight. Clouds had gathered over the top of Steens Mountain and had slowly spread westward. Rain might come later, but whether it did or not, the night would be black dark because the clouds would effectively blot out the starshine.

The three men rode in silence. Dolan didn't know what was in Bud's mind. Or Royce's. Bud probably was afraid, for this was the first fight he had faced except the one at the gate when his father had been shot. Now he knew what could happen. Before that gunfighting had been a kind of glorified adventure to him. Dolan was confident that Bud could be counted on when the blue chip was down. He was a solid kind of boy, and Joel Kendall had had a right to be proud of him as he had been proud of Sandy.

Dolan was less sure of Royce simply because he did not know the man as well as he knew Bud. The buckaroo was not one to talk about his past, but he had let it slip once that he had been through a range war in Wyoming, so a fight like this would not be new to him.

Dolan's thoughts finally turned to Sandy and himself, and he found it hard to believe what had happened during the few days since he had stood on the porch of Martin's store and watched Joel Kendall motion the three wagons into place.

At first Sandy had hated him, or pretended to. Now he wasn't sure she had, but she'd been hostile enough and they'd bumped heads. He knew so little about white women that it was impossible for him to decide why she had changed, but she had, and she had made no effort to hide it. Still, she had not thrown herself at him the way Liz Farrel had. He respected her for that. Perhaps it was one of the reasons he loved her.

He took a long, sighing breath, thinking a man gives up one thing he values to gain another. He had always believed he could do anything within reason if he set his mind to it, and now he was very certain he could be a cattleman.

He had a lot to learn, of course, but Whooper Bill and Jay Royce could teach him. He could get along with Bud and that was important. It was not a question of being right or wrong about the future, of whether he had made a mistake; it was a proposition of accepting what had happened and making the most of it. He could not go back. In that regard he was like Bronc Farrel.

The darkness was so complete that Dolan would have ridden past the turnoff to F Ranch if he had not seen the faint gleam of lamplight in the ranch house. He said, "We'll leave the horses here and walk in." They dismounted and, leading their horses into a scattering of juniper trees, tied them.

"No talking when we get to the house," Dolan said. "If some or all of the crew have got back and are in the bunkhouse, we may run into a hornet's nest. If that happens, we'll light a shuck for the horses and get back to camp. If not, we'll get Farrel. We're going to settle it tonight."

"What happens if we take him alive?" Royce asked. "And Larkin, too?"

"We'll hang 'em," Dolan said. "Larkin for Joel's murder, and Farrel for both Joel's and Bud's pa. He didn't kill them personally, but he's responsible. He's never made the slightest pretense of staying inside the law. Neither will we."

"How do we work it?" Bud asked.

"I'm going into the house," Dolan answered. "You stay at the front door. Royce, you circle the house and take the back door. I'll give you three minutes to get there. Don't let anybody out of the house. I don't care who it is."

They walked through the darkness toward the ranch house, moving noiselessly along the dusty lane until they reached the row of Lombardy poplars. "Three minutes," Dolan whispered. "We'll wait here."

"It won't take me that long," Royce said, and disappeared into the darkness.

The front door was open and lamplight fell across the front yard from the doorway and the two windows. Dolan heard voices raised in anger, Larkin's first and then Farrel's.

"You've been dogging it too long," Larkin said. "Even the men are talking about it. You've had a reputation of being a tough bird, claiming you were never going to let anyone settle on F Ranch range, but these people have been down there for days and you haven't done a god-damn thing about it. What's the matter with you, Bronc? Are you afraid of Dolan?"

"He's a good man to be afraid of," Farrel shouted back. "We never ran into a man like him before."

"I should have strung him up the first time I met him," Larkin snarled, "and not talked to you about him. But no, you were going to be cute about it. You'd hire him, you said. He was the kind of man you wanted on your side."

"He was and is," Farrel shot back. "If I had a few men like him instead of bunglers like you and Willie Martin, I wouldn't have anything to worry about."

"Don't call me a bungler," Larkin raged. "If you'd followed my advice—"

"If I'd followed your advice, the Indians would have killed all of us," Farrel said bitterly. "You're the one who tangled with Dolan in the first place and all you got was a kick in the rear end. You're the one who thought of the fence, which didn't do the trick when Dolan came along. You're the one who started to beat up the Paiute kid for no reason except you hated Paiutes. One more antic like these and you're fired."

"Don't fire me till I get Dolan," Larkin said. "Now are you going with me or not? If you're not, I'm going alone. I'll rip that camp apart as soon as it's light enough for me to start shooting."

Dolan had worked his way across the yard, Bud a step behind him. The three minutes had passed. Now Dolan stepped up on the porch. He had one brief glimpse of the two men through a window. They stood in the center of the room facing each other, their faces red with anger. He glided past and stood against the wall between the window and the door.

He would take Farrel first, then Larkin, and if Larkin smoked him down, it would be up to Bud or Royce to get the foreman. He was not concerned about having to hang them. They'd go for their guns the instant he made his appearance.

He eased along the wall toward the door, hoping there was not a loose board in the porch floor that would squeak under one of his boots. He lifted his gun from leather and let it drop back gently as he heard Farrel say, "All right, I'll go with you. If Dolan's not there, we'll ride west and circle the lakes and meet the others coming south from Hodig's store. We'll turn this country over till we find Dolan."

"Let's start," Larkin said. "We've waited too long."

"No, it's a long time till daylight. And understand one thing. You're not going down there and just start shooting at the camp."

"Because your wife's probably there with Dolan?" Larkin jeered. "Hell, Bronc, you've lost her. Don't you savvy that?"

"I'm not going to let you murder the women," Farrel said hotly. "My wife's got nothing to do with it. If you kill those women, we will have a U.S. marshal in here."

Dolan reached the door. He motioned for Bud to come on, then he moved swiftly into the room. Larkin stood where he had been, his back to Dolan. Farrel was not in sight. He must have gone into the kitchen for something.

"I'm here, Larkin," Dolan said. "You can get me without riding to Antelope Spring."

The foreman wheeled, his mouth springing open in shocked surprise, then he clawed for his gun. Dolan's right hand brought his Colt up and clear of leather in a smooth, swift draw before Larkin's .45 was out of the holster. He fired, and through the drifting cloud of powder smoke saw Larkin reel under the driving impact of the heavy slug and back up a step and then go down in a crashing fall across a chair and onto the floor.

"The lamp, Rafe," Bud yelled from the doorway behind Dolan. "You're a sitting duck for that son of a bitch."

Dolan was already diving toward the oak table that held the lamp. He blew it out and dropped flat on the floor just as a gun roared from somewhere inside the kitchen, the bullet splintering a leg of the table. Bud, coming through the door, threw a shot at Farrel, and a few seconds later Royce shouted, "We've got him between us."

Dolan swore. Royce should not have given himself away.

Now Farrel wouldn't attempt to go out through the back. He'd try for a window and run for the corral.

Dolan said, "Bud, where are you?"

"IIcrc," the boy said. "We've got him bottled, ain't we?"

"Stay here and see the cork stays in the bottle," Dolan said, "and don't shoot Royce."

He ran out of the house and turned to his left because that was the side of the house closest to the corral. If Farrel went the other way, they would lose him in the darkness. He heard a window go up just after he rounded the corner. He had guessed right. The bedrooms were on this side. It had taken Farrel these few seconds to move through the kitchen and across the bedroom.

Dolan fired three times in the direction of the window that he had heard open, then stopped and moved cautiously along the wall, not sure what had happened. He had spread his shots and he thought he had hit Farrel, but he couldn't be sure.

He was about halfway along the wall to the rear corner when Royce yelled from the back corner of the house, "He must have got away, Dolan. I don't think he's in the house." A gun roared from a few feet in front of Dolan, the shot aimed at Royce. He must have panicked and fired at the sound of the cowboy's voice.

Dolan used his last load, shooting at the gun flash. He leaped forward, holding his revolver up so he could use the barrel as a club. He stumbled over the cowman's body. Turning, he dropped to his knees and put his hands on Farrel, who lay on his back under the window. There was no movement in him.

"He's here," Dolan said.

He struck a match and held it close to Farrel's face. The rancher was dead, a bullet in his brain. A moment later Bud and Royce were there.

"It's over," Dolan said. "If we'd done this sooner, Joel might be alive."

"And we might be dead," Bud said. "No, if Grandpa was alive, he'd say this was the right way to do it."

"Maybe so," Dolan said. "Get his feet, Bud. Let's take him inside. Royce, shut the back door. We'll go in through the front and lay him beside Larkin. It's not our job to fix them for burying, but we don't want to leave him out here for the coyotes to chew on."

Later as they walked back through the darkness to their horses, Dolan told himself it was indeed over. Liz would stay on F Ranch for a while, at least until she could sell it. She would be able to keep the crew, or most of them anyhow, and out of them she would pick a new foreman. She had told him that if she owned F Ranch, there would be no trouble over Antelope Spring. He believed her.

He thought again as he had when he left camp that a man gives up something of value to gain something he values even more. It would be, he thought, a very good bargain.

How many of these Dell bestsellers have you read?

The Naked Ape by Desmond Morris   95c

Nicholas and Alexandra by Robert K. Massie $1.25

The Tower of Babel by Morris L. West $1.25

Pretty Maids All In A Row by Francis Pollini   95c

Jefferson Square by Noel Gerson   95c

The Brand Name Calorie Counter by Corinne T. Netzer   95c

The Survivors by Anne Edwards   95c

The Doctor's Quick Weight-Loss Diet
by I. Maxwell Stillman M.D., and S. Sinclair Baker   95c

Stop-Time by Frank Conroy   95c

The Deal by G. William Marshall   95c

The Gospel Singer by Harry Crews   95c

Horse Under Water (A Putnam Book) by Len Deighton   75c

Three Into Two Won't Go by Andrea Newman   95c

The Ginger Man by J. P. Donleavy   95c

The Monkey Puzzle Tree by Nona Coxhead   95c

The Operating Theater by Vincent Brome   95c

Soul On Ice (A Delta Edition) by Eldridge Cleaver $1.95

If you cannot obtain copies of these titles at your local bookseller, just send the price (plus 10c per copy for handling and postage) to Dell Books, Box 2291, Grand Central Post Office, New York, N.Y. 10017. No postage or handling charge is required on any order of five or more books.

BREAK THE YOUNG LAND 50c
Joshua Stark

THE HARDY BREED 50c
Giles A. Lutz

RIDERS OF THE BUFFALO GRASS 50c
Bliss Lomax

A GUN FOR JOHNNY DEERE 50c
Wayne D. Overholser

THE GUNS OF JUDGMENT DAY 50c
Cliff Farrell

NO GOD IN SAGUARO 50c
Lewis B. Patten

RECKONING AT RIMBOW 45c
Norman A. Fox

THE BLEEDING LAND 50c
Giles Lutz

SHADOW MOUNTAIN 50c
Bliss Lomax

SHADOW OF A HAWK 50c
Michael Bonner

SHOTGUN BOTTOM 50c
Bill Burchardt

SUMMER OF THE SIOUX 50c
Wayne D. Overholser

THE VANQUISHED 50c
Brian Garfield

MIKE SHAYNE MYSTERIES
by Brett Halliday

More than 30 million Mike Shayne mysteries have been printed in Dell Book editions alone!

DATE WITH A DEAD MAN 45c

DIE LIKE A DOG 45c

MURDER TAKES NO HOLIDAY 45c

IN A DEADLY VEIN 50c

MARKED FOR MURDER 50c

SO LUSH SO DEADLY 50c

THIS IS IT MIKE SHAYNE 50c

VIOLENCE IS GOLDEN 50c

Frank Yerby's magnificent historical

novels have enthralled millions around the world. . . .

Don't miss —

Captain Rebel

A story of the daring exploits of the Confederate blockade runners. Tyler Meredith is Mr. Yerby's rebel captain—a rebel against the United States as he runs guns and supplies for the Confederacy.

Fairoaks

In a big, surging novel that ranges from an aristocratic southern plantation to the slave markets of Africa, Frank Yerby creates his most unforgettable character—a man who could never chain his own fierce hungers.   75c

Floodtide

A novel which dramatically portrays the human, as well as the economic, side of slavery and the embittered controversy which finally erupted into a terrible Civil War.   75c

Jarrett's Jade

Cruel, relentless, daring, James Jarrett fulfilled his most passionate desires first with a yielding blonde beauty, then with a fiery, maddeningly sensual slave girl—only to face a choice no man should have to make.   75c